ESCAPE FROM MURDER

A bungalow filled with hunting trophies is the background for a brutal murder. Dr Ian Jax has reason to believe his sister is somehow involved. She denies having visited the bungalow, although there were several witnesses. In desperation, Dr Jax calls in his friend, Bill Rice, a private detective. As Bill soon discovers, there are many candidates for the role of murderer. He finally finds the criminal — but not before danger and excitement appear on the scene.

MARGUERITE STAND

ESCAPE FROM MURDER

Complete and Unabridged

LINFORD
Leicester

First published in Great Britain in 1965 by
Robert Hale Limited
London

First Linford Edition
published 2003
by arrangement with
Robert Hale Limited
London

British Library CIP Data

Stand, Marguerite
    Escape from murder.—Large print ed.—
Linford mystery library
    1. Detective and mystery stories
    2. Large type books
    I. Title
    823.9'14 [F]

LINCOLNSHIRE
COUNTY COUNCIL

    ISBN 0–7089–9971–9

Published by
F. A. Thorpe (Publishing)
Anstey, Leicestershire

Set by Words & Graphics Ltd.
Anstey, Leicestershire
Printed and bound in Great Britain by
T. J. International Ltd., Padstow, Cornwall

This book is printed on acid-free paper

For
LOU,
the best sister
in the world.

1

I slipped the letter out of my pocket and read it through again, wondering as I did so why its contents worried me so much. It wasn't even as if it came from Gwenda. And yet it was partly because of Gwenda that I was making this journey. She had seemed different last time I saw her. There was something about her — a vague sort of sadness which I could not define. *Gwenda* sad? Always as children we had romped together, sharing escapades and toys and sweets. We had been closer than most brothers and sisters, perhaps chiefly because Gwenda was somewhat of a tomboy.

Then we grew up and I went to university — the first stage towards my ambition of becoming a doctor. Gwenda went to college and afterwards became secretary to the managing director of a large electrical firm in Cleand, a town some miles from home. At first we wrote regularly to each other, sharing every new experience. Then after a time our letters became less frequent and we seemed to drift apart.

How far apart I began to realize now, sitting in this small café with Tiny Bullen's letter in my hand. Six months ago Gwenda had returned home. When I saw her shortly afterwards she had volunteered no explanation for her decision to give up her job and go back home. And, sensing that she did not want to give any reason, I asked no questions.

Thinking about it now I realised how strange it was that there should be any sort of reserve between us. I seemed to see again Gwenda's eyes — still dark and lovely but with that inexplicable sadness . . . As if she had a secret which she could share with no one, not even me . . .

I lifted my coffee cup and started to sip the half-cold liquid . . .

Back in my car and heading for home again, I was thinking about Gwenda and yet Tiny Bullen's letter had been about my parents — not my sister.

'I feel you should know that your

mother and father are not well. Your sister seems to be worried about them, and I think you should come home and see for yourself the way things are.'

The way things are . . . A typical 'Bullen' statement. He was our local busybody and knew far more about other folks' business than they knew themselves. When I first received his note I was angry. Why should this meddling chatterbox tell me what to do?

I had thrust the piece of paper into my wallet and for a whole day tried to forget it. But, during brief intervals between examining one patient and the next I kept remembering . . . kept thinking . . .

'Your sister seems to be worried about them . . . '

Was Gwenda worried about them or about something else?

'Your mother and father are not well . . . '

But we had always been a disgustingly healthy family, all four of us. Why should Mum and Dad both be unwell now? Just when Gwenda was home to give them a helping hand . . .

I had reached the end of the by-pass, and as I began to drive along the country roads which would soon lead me to my home, I was starting to laugh at my fears. After all, it was stupid to have chucked up everything and raced away from the hospital like this. Mum and Dad possibly both had a touch of 'flu which was not serious enough for Gwenda to write about. Perhaps I had imagined that she was different last time I saw her — had imagined that look in her eyes.

Yet as I got nearer home I knew quite certainly it was only one phrase in that letter bringing me home. If Gwenda was *showing* her worry, then there must be something very wrong — and I could *not* believe it was anything to do with my parents. Quite possibly Bullen had put his own construction on my sister's anxious appearance.

My thoughts switched over to him as I approached Mewsdale. He had earned his nickname because he was long and lanky. Right from my boyhood I could remember him as almost part of the small town where I grew up. His gaunt lugubrious face matched his profession for he was assistant to our local undertaker.

The very last time I was home he had stopped me and asked me a host of questions about where I was now, what I did, and hoped to do. And at last, wanting to escape, I had suggested he must be busy and would not want me to delay him. 'Oh, no, you won't hinder me,' he had said, 'I'm retired now.'

'Roseville' was a tiled, six-roomed cottage set back from the road. I halted my car at the gate and, climbing out, glanced up at the bedroom windows. The curtains were drawn across my parents' window, although it was well past eleven in the morning. For no reason at all fear came tumbling back into my brain. No reason at all — except that the curtains of my parents' room were across the window and I could never remember such a thing, day or night, for all my life. Even when she went to bed Mother left them undrawn. 'I love to watch the moon and stars before I go to sleep,' she used to say.

With her words echoing in my mind I reached the door and turned the handle, but even before I stepped into the house I think I knew . . .

Gwenda came out of the kitchen door at the further end of the passage. She was obviously startled to see me. 'You came quickly! I only sent the telegram two hours ago,' she said. Her voice was expressionless and she put out her hand to touch the wall as she came towards me, almost as if she felt dizzy and was trying to steady herself.

'I must have left the hospital before your wire got there,' I said. 'I had a letter from Tiny Bullen telling me that Mum and Dad were unwell and that you were worried about them.'

For a second anger sparked up in her eyes. I thought she was going to denounce the man for interfering, but all she said was, 'He's always been an old woman for gossiping. He's worse than ever now he's retired.'

As she spoke she was moving towards the living room. She sat down slowly in a chair by the fireside, although there was no fire in the grate. I stood looking down at her, the coldness of the room seeming to eat into me until I was no more than a block of ice. I could not move, could not speak, could not think . . .

At last she spoke but there was no need for her to tell me. I remembered my mother from a few months ago as healthy and full of life. Now she was dead.

I do not fear death. Although all my life is dedicated to fighting it I know that, ultimately, it is an enemy who must win. But to realize that my own mother had been taken from me, and that all my skill could be of no avail, that she had died and I had not even known she was ill . . . it was more than I could bear.

I said, 'Why didn't you wire me before? You know I would have come.'

Gwenda looked up at me and I knew I had not imagined the sadness in her eyes. It was still there, only now it was intensified a hundred times. Sadness and something else . . . Regret? Fear? I did not know.

I wanted to ask her, 'What is the matter, Gwenda? There is something — something even more than Mother's death — something I can't understand.

Confide in me, Gwenda — tell me what is wrong.' But I stood there looking at her and I said nothing.

She dropped her glance from mine and turned to look into the empty grate. She said, 'What I have got to tell you, Ian — it will be a shock. Perhaps it would be better if you sat down.' I moved awkwardly to the nearest chair but almost before I was in it she had told me the ugly truth. Mother had taken her own life.

'But why?' I demanded. 'She had so much to live for. She was always so *happy*.'

'But not lately,' Gwenda said. 'Since I have been home she has been different. Father has too.' The name roused me and I got up quickly from the chair. 'Where is Dad?' I asked.

Gwenda stood up too, and walked across to the french door. Then she paused. 'He's in the garden,' she said. 'Will you go to him first?'

I thought that would be best, but as I made to open the door she looked up at me. 'Don't let him see you are distressed,' she pleaded. 'The last few hours have put years on him, Ian. Somehow he seems like an old man.' She was trying to prepare me for the shock, but she did not succeed. How can anyone be prepared for a shock like that? When I had seen my father last he had been an upright statue of a man. Now he was slumped on a bench at the bottom of the garden, his shoulders hunched, his hands held limply on his knees. He was painfully thin.

He glanced up when he heard my footstep. His face was lined and haggard. He looked through me rather than at me, and he gave no sign that he was glad to see me — or even that he knew I was there. I sat down on the bench at his side and, because there seemed to be nothing I could say, nothing I could do to ease the grief that was his, I took one of his hands in mine and held it there.

He appeared not to notice and for several moments I stayed looking down at the hand I knew so well. Like my own, it was a doctor's hand. Father was a G.P. in Mewsdale, the small town where we had always lived — while my ambition was to become a consultant at a modern hospital. I had almost attained that ambition. But, sitting there in the garden of my home that day with my father broken and grief-stricken beside me, the dream I had cherished for so long faded. I knew what I must do.

I said gently, releasing his hand, 'I'll give up the consultant idea, Dad, and become your partner.' He seemed suddenly to realize I was there but not to grasp the meaning of my words. He said, 'Your mother, Ian. Has Gwenda told you that . . . ' His voice, trembling and uncertain, trailed off into silence. I tried to swallow the lump in my throat, to force back the tears which stung my eyes. I stood up and walked slowly into the house.

★   ★   ★

Afterwards I thought it strange that I had not tried to comfort my father that day. Perhaps I believed that the promise to come home as his partner would console him more than anything else I could do. If so I was quite wrong, for the fact that I was there, sharing his work, made no difference at all. Of course I helped him physically, doing most of the visiting while he took surgery and attended only uncomplicated cases.

But mentally I could not help him in the smallest way. He withdrew into a lonely self-made prison of grief, and neither Gwenda nor I could reach him.

Gwenda was relieved when I had settled up my affairs at the hospital and returned home. She now had a secretarial post in the town — certainly not such a well-paid position as she had in Cleand, but she seemed to like it quite well. Yet at times I still saw that sad look in her eyes and, although we appeared outwardly to share a happy companionship, I knew that something was wrong. There was some inexplicable barrier between us which, no matter how hard I tried, I could not penetrate.

It was Tiny Bullen who first told me about what had happened at The Elms, a bungalow on the other side of the town.

I was coming out of Mr Underhill's gate. The old man was ninety-three, and had scalded a hand rather badly. I attended to the injury and told him the nurse would have to go regularly to dress it. I was sorry he had hurt himself but I always liked a chat with him. He was a colourful character and, although he had never been further than the next town, knew a great deal about many things and could converse freely on almost any subject under the sun. Having lived all his life in Mewsdale, he knew the family histories of most of the townsfolk. But unlike Tiny Bullen, he asked no questions and curiosity was not one of his vices.

Now as I walked down the path from the old man's door Tiny came out of the next house. I guessed he had been waiting inside for me to emerge. 'Oh, Doctor,' he said, hurrying towards me. 'I'm sorry if Mr Underhill is ill again. Is it anything serious?'

Doctors do not talk about their patients and so, evading the question, I side-stepped with, 'I'm glad to see *you* looking so well, Mr Bullen.'

'If I am it's a marvel to be sure. I don't *feel* up to much — not since I helped Mrs

Letts' new lodger move in over there. Like I said to her — what did she want to get herself a lodger for when . . . ' But the end of his remark was lost. I had reached the car and my slam of the door drowned his last words. But he was undeterred. With a hand on the open window he bent down to say, 'Had it all redecorated too — and was afraid she wouldn't get it cleaned up before the carpets arrived. Carpets!'

I let in the clutch. Tiny was still talking as my Consul moved away. I could hear his voice repeating, 'Carpets! Why in the name of justice should Mrs Letts want those?' I smiled to myself. What connection was there between justice and carpets for Mrs Letts' bungalow? If I had known that day all I know now I might not have thought it so funny.

I told Gwenda about it over tea that afternoon. Father was out on a case and we knew he would not be back till evening. First of all my sister, too, was amused. But towards the end of the meal, a portion of teacake halfway to her mouth, she said suddenly, 'It *is* strange that Mrs Letts should be having her place redecorated and carpets laid. The bungalow has always been a disgrace. The paint flaked off the outside of it years ago, and the front door looked almost off its hinges the last time I went along Rook Lane.'

'Perhaps she has won the pools,' I grinned.

'Yes,' Gwenda agreed, 'or perhaps Madeline has.' Madeline . . . I had nearly forgotten she ever existed. Yet we had gone to school together, and she had joined in some of our childish pranks when brought by her mother to our house during the holidays. But she had never been one of us . . .

I said slowly, 'Do you remember how she used to boast about the number of public houses her mother had visited in one weekend?'

'Yes. Mr Bullen says that Mrs Letts never goes now — but Madeline does.'

'Is it just the two of them in the bungalow now?' I asked.

'Yes — unless it's true that they have a lodger as you say.'

'As Tiny Bullen says,' I corrected her.

'I don't believe they have ever let rooms before,' Gwenda remarked, 'but I suppose if Mr Bullen says this it's right . . . '

The expression in her voice made me reply, 'You don't like Tiny any more now than when we were kids, do you? *Then* you used to run the other way if you saw him coming.'

'You were a boy,' she answered, and I saw her fingers tighten on the handle of her cup as she spoke. 'He never touched you, but whenever I met him he used to put his bony fingers under my chin, and always it gave me the creeps.' She dropped her cup with a small crash into its saucer then, getting hastily up from the table, she ran from the room.

I went after her, cursing myself for a fool. Yet how could I have known that talking about Tiny Bullen would upset her so much? Gwenda had thrown herself on her bed and was sobbing bitterly when I reached her bedroom door. I went across and put my hand on her shoulder. 'I'm sorry, old girl,' I said. 'I didn't mean to upset you.'

She looked up at me, her face wet with

tears, her make-up smudged. 'It's not your fault,' she said. 'I keep thinking it might be mine. I keep wondering if it was because of me that Mum . . . '

I gave her shoulder a little shake, puzzling as I did so what connection there was, if any, between our recent conversation and Mother's death.

'Don't be so stupid,' I said, but I could not console her. That unhappy shadow was back in her eyes again. I slipped my arm under her shoulder and raised her into a sitting position. Then I sat down on the bed beside her. 'Listen, Gwenda,' I said, 'you mustn't torture yourself like this. You must know that it is silly to blame yourself. I could do the same, I suppose. I could be partly to blame for not coming home more often. I have blamed myself for not coming as soon as I got Tiny's letter. If I had been here, I say to myself . . . But it's no good, Gwenda. We can't alter things now. We have just got to forget the past and live for the present.'

She rested her face against my shoulder. 'I know you are right, Ian,' she said. 'I will try not to be so stupid again.'

She stood up and went across to the dressing table to repair her damaged make-up. I went back to the dining room and began to remove the things from the tea table. Automatically I carried out cups and plates, not really thinking what I was doing. The question was whirling round in my brain again — the question which had haunted me for a long time now. Why had Mother taken her own life? Why? *Why?*

2

A week later I had completely forgotten Tiny's information about the bungalow. Even Gwenda's outburst had faded from my mind. Life was very full, for I was gradually taking over more and more of my father's work. That afternoon when I arrived home after visiting two very difficult cases Gwenda met me in the hall.

'Dad's gone up to bed,' she told me. 'That means you will have to take surgery tonight . . . '

I had been looking forward to an evening with my feet up, watching my favourite television series, and hoping there would not be too many low-flying aircraft over to interfere with my enjoyment. But relaxation was not to be mine after all.

'I'll go up and have a word with Dad before we start tea,' I said. 'I hope he is not going to be really ill . . . '

'I have a tray ready for him,' Gwenda

said. 'Will you carry it up with you?'

I had slipped out of my coat and hung it up just in time to take the tray from her.

'If he's asleep I wouldn't wake him,' she said. 'He went up just as soon as I came in this evening. I tried to persuade him to take a book with him and read for a while, but he said he had a headache and only wanted to be quiet . . . '

But Dad was not asleep when I gently pushed open the door with my toe. 'Is that you, Ian?' he asked.

I rested the tray on one hand for a moment and touched the electric switch with the other. He blinked in the sudden light.

I was startled afresh at the thinness of his face, the dullness of his eyes. He had always been such an active man, both physically and mentally. Like myself, he had taken an interest in every kind of sport and was a very avid reader. But since Mother's death he had lost interest in everything. It was as if life had ceased to have any meaning for him.

I put the tray down on a table by his

bed. For a few moments I wondered whether I ought to speak sternly to him, tell him he must force himself out of this apathy, this defeat. And then, standing there, looking down at him, a strange thought came to me. Several months ago when I sat beside him in the garden I had been suddenly convinced I must give up my hospital ambition and come home to help him.

Now, all at once, I was equally convinced that it was not *only* my mother's death which was making him ill. I do not know why the thought came to me. Perhaps it was some sort of telepathy between a father and son who had always been very close. I said, 'What's worrying you, Dad? It might help if you told someone, you know.'

He sat up in bed, not looking at me, and reached for the tray. I moved it on to the bed for him and waited while he drank the tea and started on the dainty egg and cress sandwiches which Gwenda had prepared. I wanted to say something more to break the awkward silence which was there between us, cutting us off from each other. It was my father who spoke first. He said, 'I thought you knew, Ian. Your mother and I were everything to one another. I just can't — forget.' He still did not look at me and I knew that his words were only half the truth. I cannot explain why I was so certain, but from that afternoon I knew my father was keeping something from me.

Turning to go back downstairs, I felt suddenly lonely. Perhaps it was that new feeling of loneliness which made me accept so willingly the offer of friendship which was made to me in the surgery that evening.

There was the usual crop of sore throats, blood pressures, and the rest. Some patients were talkative, others reticent — all of them I knew. Until the last one.

He knocked loudly on the door before he opened it and stepped into my consulting room. He was tall with fair hair above a bronzed complexion, and his left hand was swathed in a white rag. He sat down in the chair opposite my own and rested the hand on the desk between us. He said, 'I've cut it rather badly, Doctor — think it may need a stitch or two.'

I tugged off the soiled and homemade bandage asking him, as I did so, how it had happened.

'It was the eagle,' he said.

'Eagle?' I repeated, not comprehending.

'Yes, I hunt a great deal — in Africa, you know. I have many souvenirs of my journeys — stuffed animals which I have shot, birds I have captured. The eagle is — was — in a glass case. I was moving it and put him temporarily on a small table. Other things were on the floor, dumped there by the carriers. I was bending over to pick some of them up when that stupid Bullen fellow came along and knocked the eagle over.'

'Ah,' I said, more to myself than to him, 'Mr Bullen . . . '

He was going on, 'The glass smashed against a packing case as it fell. Automatically I tried to save it but only succeeded in getting cut by the jagged glass.'

I had examined the wound, decided it was not bad enough to need stitches, and was now starting to bandage it.

My receptionist had been unable to find a card for this patient among my records and so I did not know his name. I said, 'You are a newcomer to this district?'

'Yes, I have just moved into 'The Elms' in Rook Lane.'

'The Elms' — Mrs Letts' bungalow which had been repainted and laid with carpets — obviously for this man. I looked at him with new interest. How had he persuaded someone like Mrs Letts to spend money on paint and wallpaper when she had not bothered about her home for years?

I asked, 'Was the eagle damaged when its glass case was smashed?'

'Not seriously thank goodness. There is a tiny bit chipped off the beak and a few feathers loosened from one wing. Fortunately the man who looks after my trophies is coming down from London next week. He examines them every year and I thought it would be a good idea if he looked at them when I was really settled in just in case anything got damaged by the move.'

I had finished bandaging his hand and, standing up, he turned to go. I felt suddenly in need of conversation. I wanted him to stay and talk to me. There were no other patients in the waiting room, no calls as far as I knew for the evening. I was in no hurry to go back to Gwenda. Both she and my father puzzled me — and here was an opportunity to forget them for a while.

I said, 'Your way of life sounds very enthralling to a G.P. in a country town like Mewsdale.'

'Oh yes? It has its moments, I'll admit, and Africa is a wonderful continent. To think that only months ago I was in the heart of it, surrounded by leopards and elephants . . . ' He seemed to come alive as he spoke, the memory of the hunt leaping to his eyes as if he could see again the animals of the jungle. I could not help contrasting his spirit with the apathy of my father. And yet my father had once been like this . . . tall, full of life, interested. Yes, once he would have been interested in this newcomer, would have wanted to know him and hear about his adventures.

The other man was saying, 'My name is Tennant — Ralph Tennant. I know doctors are busy folk but perhaps you could come along one day and see my collection?'

'I would very much like to do that.' Eagerly I accepted his invitation. And did not know what I was doing . . .

I slept uneasily that night and woke very early the next morning. Switching on the light, I glanced at my clock and found it was only half past five. For a while I stayed there, hoping I should go off to sleep again, but it was no good and at last I decided to get up.

There was plenty of secretarial work that could only be handled by myself. I dressed as quietly as possible and crept stealthily down the stairs so that I should not wake the others. I made myself a hot drink and carried it, with a tin of biscuits, into the study which opened off the passage near the front door. Having drunk the coffee and eaten one or two biscuits, I settled down to my writing. The house was still and quiet and I got on famously. I decided I must do this sort of thing more frequently. It was so much easier than trying to concentrate with people around and constant interruptions.

Time must have flown for it seemed only a very short while before I heard the gate click and looked up to see the postman coming in with his usual batch of letters. Doctors always get plenty of post — from people wanting us to advertize their pills or disinfectant or some other commodity.

I heard Gwenda come down the stairs. Always she collected the mail from the door mat, sorted it into three piles, and put it by our breakfast plates. I heard her reach the hall. There was a pause and then the sound of tearing paper as though an envelope was being opened. She was, unusually, starting to look at her own correspondence. Well, maybe it would be a good idea if I fetched mine and dealt with it before breakfast.

I stood up and walked across the soft carpet. Gwenda had her back to me as I opened the door, but she swung round quickly. I believe if she had gone on reading her letter I should have thought no more about it — but she didn't. Almost before I stepped through the doorway she had crushed the sheet of notepaper into an invisible ball, her fingers grasped so tightly round it that her knuckles were white. For a few seconds we stood looking at one another and then she regained her composure.

'You startled me, Ian,' she said. 'I had no idea you were up yet.'

'I couldn't sleep and decided to try and catch up with my writing,' I explained. But *Gwenda* did not explain. She turned and went back up the stairs.

'I'll be down in a minute or two to get breakfast,' she said. Slowly I bent over and picked up the other letters from the floor, where they were still scattered. Carrying them into the dining room, I began to sort out my own. But I was still thinking about Gwenda, upstairs reading that letter she had not wanted me to see.

I heard her moving around in the kitchen soon afterwards and before long the three of us were sitting down to breakfast. I had expected Dad to have his in bed perhaps, but he seemed much better and I started telling him about a case I was finding difficult to diagnose.

He offered to go with me when I visited the patient that afternoon. I was surprised and pleased. It was quite a while since he had shown even a vestige of interest in the practice, which had once meant so much to him.

When we left in the Consul after lunch he seemed to enjoy the ride. I remembered the trouble I had experienced with the heater over the wash basin during last evening's surgery and I started to tell him about it. The first time I used it the water had been cold. The second time it was so hot that I almost scalded my hands. Eventually it had refused to function at all. 'It's terribly annoying,' I said. 'Isn't it time we had a reliable heating system installed in the house and surgery, Dad?'

He was silent for a few moments. Then

he replied, 'What for? That water heater has been good enough for me. It will have to be good enough for you. You just haven't learnt how to use it properly.'

'But I told you what happened last night.'

'It was all right in the morning,' he stated.

Perhaps I should have left it there, but I didn't. It seemed to me necessary that a doctor's equipment should be modern and in first-rate condition. I told Dad that I thought the whole house, including the waiting room and surgery, should be centrally heated, and that we should have hot water just at the turn of a tap night or day.

I succeeded at least in rousing him out of the indifference which had claimed him for so long. He turned angrily towards me. 'And who do you think is going to finance this hare-brained scheme of yours?' he demanded. I was surprised at his vehemence and I could only stammer, 'I thought . . . I thought . . . '

'You *thought*,' he broke in. 'Well, it's time you *stopped* thinking. There's no money to spare for . . . ' He broke off abruptly.

I went on driving, my eyes concentrating on the road ahead, but my brain in a whirl. Why was there no money for modernising our home? We had always been comfortably off. The practice had been a good one, with a fair share of private patients. Gwenda and I had both been well educated and there had never appeared to be any lack of funds then. *Now* we were earning.

But looking back over the recent months, I could recall other instances when Father had refused me money for small items which I had bought eventually out of my own pocket. Yet in the past he had always been a generous man . . .

His voice, apathetic again now, broke into my thoughts. 'I . . . I'm sorry, Ian. I did not mean to snap at you like that. The truth is I'm not myself lately.'

'No, I realize that, Dad. If only I could help in some way.'

He did not reply and when I stopped the Consul he was leaning back in his seat, his eyes closed. I got out and went round to unfasten the door for him. He opened his eyes, but he did not look at me as he started to climb out of the car.

On the way home we talked about the patient we had just seen and I was glad that my father's verdict coincided with my own tentative opinion, and that he really did seem to be absorbed in the case.

We were about a couple of hundred yards away from home when someone came out of it, striding away in the opposite direction. I could only see his back but I recognised him in a moment — Ralph Tennant, the man I had talked to in surgery last night. In that instant of recognition I heard my father say something. I turned into the drive and, as I did so, I felt the seat beside me jerk. I halted the car and, switching off the engine, turned to look at Dad. I was going to tell him about Tennant and his interesting life in African jungles, but words died on my lips. My father was slumped back in the passenger seat, his face white, his body limp. He had fainted.

I told myself minutes later as I dashed towards the house that was only to be expected. He did not eat enough for a sparrow these days. I was surprised, when I turned the handle, to find the door locked. It was Gwenda's half-day, and I knew she had not intended to go out.

I banged loudly on the knocker but it was several seconds before she opened the door. Although I was worried about Dad, I could not help noticing the high colour on her cheeks, the brightness of her eyes. I said quickly, 'Dad's fainted. He has come round, but we will have to help him indoors.'

'Dad? Fainted!' There was incredulity in her voice. Neither of us could remember such a thing happening before.

'We shall have to make him eat more in future,' I told her as we made our way back to the car. He looked better now and was already starting to climb out of his seat. We got him indoors and into his chair by the fire, and Gwenda went to fetch some blankets to wrap round him. He seemed not to notice her — or me. He just sat gazing into the fire, his hands resting on the arms of his chair.

I said at last, 'Shall I take surgery again this evening, Dad?'

He looked up then. 'Yes, yes. Of course. Silly of me. I'd quite forgotten about that . . . '

Later, when surgery was over, I went back into the sitting room. Gwenda was waiting for me. 'Dad has gone to bed,' she told me. 'I have got the milk on for your coffee. Would you like me to toast something for you?'

Not many minutes afterwards I was sitting down to the poached eggs she had done for me and, picking up the salt cellar, discovered it was empty.

'More salt wanted,' I said, handing it to her. She was filling it when I remembered Ralph Tennant and asked, 'By the way, what did Mr Tennant want this afternoon?'

Her hand shook. The white grains of salt spilled over the tablecloth. 'Upset salt, upset sorrow, the old saying goes,' I commented. She screwed the top on the container and put the condiment set in front of me before she replied. Then she said, 'Who is Mr Tennant?' She spoke casually, but she had turned away from me. She went to sit down in a chair by the fire, and I could not see her face.

'He is the new lodger at Mrs Letts' and he came to the surgery last evening,' I explained. 'He'd cut his hand on some glass . . . ' I paused, putting a portion of toast into my mouth and eating it before I added, 'He was just going out of the gate today when Dad and I returned but, with Dad fainting like that, I have forgotten all about it till now.'

'Oh, *that* fellow. He didn't tell me his name. Just said he wanted to see you. Then, when I told him you were out, he said he had invited you to see some stuffed animals he had brought back from Africa or somewhere. He wanted to know when you would be accepting his invitation.'

'He said he would phone . . . Anyway, what did you tell him?'

'That he would have to see you himself — or phone . . . '

'He seems an interesting sort of chap,' I volunteered.

'I don't find it interesting to hunt and kill,' my sister answered, speaking the words slowly with a kind of reluctant emphasis on the last one. But after all she is a woman — and women are notoriously squeamish over death.

I was as unprepared for what happened next as I had been for Dad's outburst that afternoon. Gwenda got up from her chair and swung round to face me. 'You may as well know he asked *me* to go with you to see his beastly animals. Well, I'm not agreeing to do that, and if *you* go to his place you are not to ask him back here. I'll not even appear friendly to someone who makes money from the suffering of animals.' She turned and went quickly from the room, closing the door behind her.

Getting up from the table, I went to sit by the fire. I gazed into the burning coals as my father had done earlier that day. But I could not find any solution to the problems which perplexed me. No matter how long I stayed there I should never find answers to the many questions which kept thrusting into my mind.

What had been in that letter of Gwenda's this morning? Why was she so upset because Ralph Tennant had invited her into his home? What was the real reason for my father's apathy and failing health? Did *he* know why my mother had committed suicide?

One after another, like leaves forced over and over in the cruel water of a weir, the thoughts tumbled round in my mind. The ringing of the telephone shattered them and I got up to answer it. I was relieved to find it was an urgent call, and that I would have to go out at once. Attending to someone else's troubles, I could perhaps forget my own.

I did not see Gwenda again till the next morning. Unlike the previous morning, I slept much later and she was already preparing breakfast when I got down. I stood in the kitchen doorway for a moment, watching her and enjoying the delicious aroma of frying bacon. She looked up at me. 'Good morning, Ian,' she said, and then, 'I'm sorry I was so angry yesterday. Perhaps I will come with you to see Mr Tennant's trophies after all. It might be quite pleasant to see Madeline again . . .'

She went on with her task of cutting bread and butter. I said, 'You weren't really worried about *Tennant*, were you? I know it's no business of mine, but something in that letter yesterday upset you, and you didn't get over it all day. I know you so well, old girl — it's not much good trying to hide your feelings from me.'

She sliced some tomatoes and dropped them into the sizzling bacon fat before she replied. Then she said, 'You are quite wrong, Ian. That letter was from an old friend.'

'Someone I've met?'

'No. She wants me to go and see her next week. I was startled because you appeared so suddenly when I thought you were still asleep. That's all there was to it.' It sounded a plausible excuse. The only trouble was that Gwenda was such a darned poor liar.

And she didn't come with me to the Letts' bungalow after all. On the afternoon I made up my mind to go there her boss had an unexpected batch of typing in, and asked her to work overtime.

3

It was my half-day. I had told our daily woman where I should be in case of any emergency and she would contact me, if necessary.

I left my car just inside the gate of The Elms and walked across the gravelled drive. It was an attractive bungalow. Roofed with red tiles, it had two gables over the wide bow windows on either side of the door, which opened almost as soon as I had knocked.

Tennant said cordially, 'Come in, come in.' As I stepped inside he added, 'I'm disappointed you haven't brought your sister. I saw her the other afternoon and asked her if she would come too.'

He closed the door behind me. 'Your sister seems a nice kid,' he told me.

'Gwenda is not exactly a kid, as you put it,' I replied.

'Oh dear — no offence meant. She's a nice girl, if you prefer that word.' He glanced at me. I had the odd feeling he was waiting for me to react. To what?

I said, 'Yes, I can agree with you. One boy and one girl in a family sometimes fight like a dog and cat — not myself and Gwenda. We have always been very close.'

Until lately . . . But I did not add that qualification.

He laughed. 'So when you acquire a brother-in-law he would have to measure up to pretty high standards, eh?' He was apparently amused, yet again I had the feeling that he was waiting for my reaction. Then I thought, 'he's trying to hint that he wouldn't mind being in the running for position as my brother-in-law — even though he has only just met Gwenda . . .' Was there such a thing as love at first sight? Anyway some hopes for him! If only he could have seen my sister the other afternoon, if only he could have heard her saying she would have nothing to do with him . . . a hunter . . .

I could hear a murmur of voices from the room to my left, but Tennant did not lead the way in there. He gestured towards the walls of the wide passage.

Alligators, stuffed but looking ferociously alive, snarled down at me — big ones, smaller ones. Springbok horns, a tiger's head, a lion's, looking so life-like that it seemed impossible the body belonging to the head was not in the room on the other side of the wall ... There were native spears too.

* * *

'Assegais,' Tennant said. 'The long javelin is for throwing, the shorter spear for stabbing at close quarters.'

'I shouldn't like to argue with anyone behind either of those,' I laughed.

On the floor was a splendid leopard skin. My companion watched me as I gazed down at it but he made no comment then. He said, 'Come on in and have a drink.'

Madeline looked up as I went into the room. She was sitting in an armchair and made no attempt to move. She might be a fashion model if her studied pose, added to her fashionable hair-do and clothes, were any guide.

'No need to introduce us,' she said. 'Ian Jax and I started our school lives in the same building. Rather detracts from the status of *Doctor* when you have been kids together.' She gave a little laugh. 'Ian isn't much like you, Ralph. Couldn't imagine you scoring twelve goals in an afternoon — but Ian was always sports crazy. You played Rugger at the university, didn't you?'

But I had no chance to reply. Tennant was frowning. 'I might not have excelled on the sports field,' he said, 'but I expect my muscles and physique are as tough and hard as his — more so probably.'

He waved his hand in the direction of the door. 'Now, that leopard skin out in the passage. That creature was a killer, and it was terrorizing a village when I happened to turn up there — oh, three years ago, I suppose that was. Two natives had already fallen victim to that leopard, the rest of them went in fear of their lives. 'You're a hunter,' they said. 'Rid us of this plague.' And I did . . . ' Tennant got really excited as he described the chase and final victory.

He walked across the room. 'See here,' he said, and I followed him to a corner. He picked up a stick from a rack there. 'That was my reward, presented with due ceremony by the chief of that village to acknowledge their thanks to me for delivering them from that killer.'

The stick he handed me was carved with inter-twining snakes. I took it from him. 'My goodness, it's a heavy thing!' I exclaimed, and looked back at the rack which held quite a lot of similar trophies, all weirdly carved with heads and symbols. 'Are they all as weighty as this one?' I asked, 'and were they all presented to you for ridding villages of killers?'

'Oh no. I made a point of collecting them. I paid for some of them with elephant tusks. Ivory is valuable coinage with the natives out there.'

Still holding the stick, I looked at Tennant. 'Which gave you the most satisfaction — the chase or the kill?' I asked.

He laughed again. 'I couldn't answer that,' he said. 'The chase is exciting . . . No, I can't tell you . . . '

'Come here and look at this picture.' A voice spoke suddenly from the other side of the room and I turned. I had not seen this other man before. Dark and slim, he was standing behind the open door and Tennant said, 'I've been terribly lacking in my duties as host. This is John Harvey. He comes regularly to look after my trophies — you know, cleans them, sees they never get moth in them . . . ' I replaced the stick, crossed the room. Harvey turned to acknowledge the introduction to me. His handshake was firm and hard, but very brief, for straightaway he swung back to look at the picture he had called us to see. He said, 'You've acquired this since I saw you last, Ralph. It's tremendously good. I heard what you were saying, Doctor — and I have a feeling it could almost be satisfying to be the victim . . . See the expression there — could it be excitement at discovering what lies beyond — death?'

Madeline's voice said, 'For goodness sake — why must you get on to a subject like death?' She shuddered.

'I'm sorry,' Harvey apologized, but he

did not look round at her.

Tennant had gone to pour us drinks. As we turned away from the picture and sat down I looked at Harvey. I remarked, 'Yours seems an odd kind of job — performing the beauty treatment of a lot of stuffed animals and birds. Do you do much of it?'

A little smile twitched his lips. 'Quite a lot,' he told me. 'I travel all over Britain, attending to all sorts of collections. But my business is in London. I have a large number of my own curios. You, as a doctor, would be interested in my collection of skulls.' Again his lips moved in what might have been intended to be a smile — but it gave his face a suddenly sinister expression.

'Most people would think it ghoulish to keep those sort of things,' he said, 'but someone like you would understand the fascination of examining and collating data about them.' He put his hand into his pocket and withdrew a small card. 'That's my address — do promise to come along one day.'

Madeline had been silently listening as

we talked. Now she roused animatedly. But I was not really interested in her. I was watching Tennant. He was a peculiar fellow — he could be very charming one moment, the next looking cross. Just now he was scowling and after a moment or two he broke into Madeline's gay chatter.

'Go and tell your mother we are ready to eat,' he ordered. 'And see it is all hot.'

Madeline gave a small pout, but she went off to obey him. As the door swung to behind her he said, 'Rolls and sausages — but I do like them to be *hot*.'

I wasn't thinking about our coming snack. I was remembering the swing of Madeline's hips, the piled blonde hair. 'I knew her when she was a youngster,' I said. 'Odd how people develop and alter.'

'The female sex more than ours,' Harvey put in. 'I'd lay ten bob to a penny that the colour of *her* hair has not always been what it is today.'

I did not answer that. It wouldn't really be fair to Madeline if I'd told him how mousey and undistinguished she had looked when I remembered her, nor that I had expected her to develop into a drab charwoman, the same as her mother. I began, 'Even if she *does* owe something to beauty preparations, Madeline Letts is rather lovely now . . . '

'Madeline Letts?' Harvey interrupted, and looked at Tennant. 'You didn't say her name was Letts.'

'Didn't I? I think nearly everyone calls her simply Madeline. Is it important?'

'No, it's just that I knew someone of that name years ago.'

Then Madeline was back again. She held open the door while Mrs Letts came in, carrying an obviously heavy tray. I stood up. I could remember the woman from when I was a boy. She had come to work for my mother and I had been 'Master Ian' to her. Then all her movements had been mercury-quick — a great contrast from the lumbering progress now of this elderly-looking woman.

As I crossed the room, intending to take the tray from her, I was thinking, there must be some reason for her obesity — diabetes perhaps?

I had almost reached her when she

47

stumbled and if I had not been there she would have dropped the tray. Madeline said crossly, 'You clumsy oaf! If it had not been for Ian, we should have lost our tea.'

I felt suddenly angry. Why should *she* be treating her own mother as a servant? I said levelly as I put the load on a table near the settee, 'This is heavy. Couldn't *you* have carried it in?'

'Me!' Madeline laughed and sat down beside John Harvey. Mrs Letts was still standing where she had been when I relieved her of the tray. I saw her glance raised slowly to her daughter — deep-set dark eyes which were filled with hate. The woman's gaze shifted to the man at Madeline's side.

And her expression changed. The hate was still there — but something else as well. Fear?

I glanced quickly towards John Harvey. But his swarthy face revealed nothing. To him she appeared the veriest stranger — uninteresting and of no importance . . .

Tennant was saying, 'Well, come on, all of you. I detest cold sausage, so I'll be tempted in a minute to forget I'm host and be starting before my guests.' Mrs Letts turned cumbrously and took her massive bulk slowly from the room. She shut the door with a thud behind her.

Tennant took the covers off two dishes. In one were sausages, in the other rolls. On a plate were small pats of butter. 'Help yourselves,' Tennant ordered. I buttered a roll and, armed with a fork, speared a sausage.

'Why not hot dogs?' Harvey asked.

'This way it tastes different,' Tennant declared. 'Oh well — perhaps because I had this fare at home before your hamburgers and the rest were heard of.' He looked at Madeline. 'By the way, John here knows someone the same name as yourself, Madeline.'

'Do you?' With a sausage half-way to her mouth, she paused. 'Do tell me who. I thought our name was ever so uncommon. I've never known anyone else with it.' She was waiting with the small-girl eagerness she could apparently assume with ease. With her mother she was no longer juvenile — but with a man it was different.

John Harvey said, 'It's a chap in my club. I don't know why I said anything. I daresay if you look in the Directory you'd find a dozen namesakes.' He glanced towards a box on the sideboard.

'Your slides in there?' he asked Tennant. He spoke casually, but I was sure he was merely changing the subject. When I had said *Letts* he had been betrayed into displaying interest. *Now* he wished he had said nothing — especially since Mrs Letts had come in. I was sure I had not mistaken the hate in her eyes. *She* had known him and *he* was acquainted with someone of her name. First of all he had said, 'Someone years ago' then 'A chap in my club'. But in reality was it Mrs Letts he had had in mind from the beginning? Yet it was none of my business . . .

And during the next hour I completely forgot the matter. We finished eating and Tennant set up his projector. Lying back, hands behind her head, Madeline watched him as he inserted the first slide.

She said, 'Working the machine is usually my job.'

'And you'll have to do it this evening when I'm out in front of an audience giving a lecture, but there's no need here . . . '

I couldn't help being fascinated. This man must have a nerve to stand photographing elephants as they charged towards him, to get close enough to picture a lioness playing with her cubs.

'Don't you find taking pictures of the animals more satisfying than killing them?' I queried.

'Satisfying? You asked me that before. *Must* there be that particular emotion attached to everything? Rogue elephants, killer leopards *have* to be destroyed. It's the law out there — you kill one life to preserve others more precious.'

The ringing of the telephone in the hall stopped our entertainment. 'You answer it,' Tennant said to Madeline.

'Oh, bother — let whoever it is think there is no one in,' she said.

'No.' I got to my feet. 'If you don't mind I'll go,' I put in. 'It might be for me.'

51

It was.

I returned to the room to make my apologies. 'I'm sorry — this is what happens,' I said ruefully. 'Tummy pains and accidents don't respect the doctor's time off.'

'You must come back and see the rest of my slides another afternoon,' Tennant said.

Although I did not know it then I was to return to 'The Elms' the very next day — but not to see his lovely pictures . . .

4

The phone, necessary but often maddening background to my life, rang when I was almost ready to go out the following morning.

'Nurse Mackail here. Can you come round to 'The Elms' in Rook Lane? Mrs Letts has had a fall.' The nurse added a couple more succinct phrases and I knew she had a serious case on her hands.

As I drove to Rook Lane my thoughts were jumping ahead to the bungalow. Mrs Letts would fall heavily with all her bulk. On the other hand, I had known several fat people who had been little the worse after a tumble — padded as they were with their plumpness.

Naturally I went to the front door but a voice inside told me, 'You'll have to go round to the back. This door is locked and there is no key.' That had been Tiny Bullen's voice — I might have guessed he

53

would be in on any excitement! Of course, from his window opposite he would have seen the nurse arrive . . .

By the time I reached the other entrance he was there, his gaunt face set in its usual gloomy lines, but his voice sounding a trifle smug as he began, '*I found her* — inside here she was . . . '

As I stepped into the kitchen it felt very warm and smelt as though something was being cooked. I guess I was a bit brusque with the man as I brushed past him, cutting into his sentence with my abrupt, 'Where is the patient?'

But he had no need to reply. I was through the kitchen and in a tiny passage now. From beyond a door to my right came the sound of Nurse Mackail's voice. 'In here, Doctor.'

I went into a dim room to find the nurse standing at the bedside. I reached for the electric switch and pressed it down, but there could have been no bulb, for the room still held its dimness. I took several quick strides towards the window to find, instead of curtains, a ragged sheet stretched across it, keeping out the light and air. I gave it a sharp pull. It tore and fell in a dirty crumpled heap at my feet. At least my action had let in some day-light and I turned back to examine my patient.

From the tone of the nurse's voice when she phoned me I had imagined Mrs Letts to be seriously injured — that there was possibly something I could do for her. But there was nothing. Even if I had flown I should not have been in time to save her.

She lay on her back. She was still fully clothed, as I had seen her yesterday. The nurse pointed to a small abrasion on Mrs Letts' head.

'She must have knocked herself on the key when she fell. She was just inside the door . . . '

It took me only a few moments to decide that the woman on the bed had died quite a long while ago, a fact which I told to Nurse Mackail.

'Oh . . . No . . . '

'You moved her. You, a nurse, must have known she was dead.'

'No — I thought I felt a flicker of her

pulse. So, as a nurse, I *had* to get her into a warm bed. I had to try to revive her. But it was useless. It's sad. It's always sad when this sort of thing happens. An old lady, alone in a house at night, and then she trips — stays for hours — and in the end dies because there is no help at hand . . . '

'*Why* was she alone?' I demanded. 'Where was her daughter?'

'I don't know — but for her sake there won't need to be any fuss, will there?'

'Fuss?' I repeated. 'You should know that in the case of a sudden death like this the police and coroner have to be informed.'

'I believe when a doctor has been attending a patient he can issue a death certificate,' she said.

'But she was *not* my patient.'

'She has been to the surgery to see your father.'

'How do you know that?'

'She told me so — she had a bad knee, and went several times . . . '

If that was true it could have caused her to trip, but not to die — and that mark on the forehead was very superficial. I was not satisfied. I began to make a detailed examination. Once Nurse Mackail asked, 'Is this necessary?'

I glanced up at her. Then I turned the body slightly and I knew for certain how Mrs Letts had died. A word formed in my mind — an ugly word — for I knew that the injury on the back of her head had not been caused by a fall. She had been struck from behind by a heavy blunt instrument . . .

Straightening, I looked across at the nurse. I stated, 'Mrs Letts was murdered — and you must have known.'

'No . . . No . . . ' Her right hand reached for one of the bedposts. She gripped it so suddenly and so firmly that I thought it was going to collapse. It was an old iron bedstead, held together in one place with string.

I put the grubby sheet over the victim's face. 'There's nothing I can do for her, but I shall have to make one or two phone calls,' I said.

In the doorway I looked back. The room, with its bare boards and grimy ceiling, might have belonged to a slum tenement. Nurse Mackail was bending over the bed . . .

I left her and went on out into the dark little passage. I paused, glancing to my right. A door there obviously led to the front part of the bungalow. I took the couple of steps necessary to reach it and turned the handle. It was as though that door separated hell from heaven — good from evil. Mrs Letts' side was dirty and unfurnished — Ralph Tennant's shining and opulent.

I had to walk over the leopard skin to reach the telephone. I was about to pick up the handset when I thought that perhaps I ought to ask permission. I had not seen Madeline or Tennant since I arrived. Where were they?

I stepped across and tapped on the door of the sitting room. There was no reply and I decided that, with or without permission, I would have to make those calls.

I got through to the police station and then returned to the back of the bungalow. The bedroom door was open.

Nurse Mackail was not there now. Quickly I went towards the kitchen. The nurse had put on her raincoat and small navy-blue hat. She said, a note of defiance in her voice, 'I have other cases to visit this morning.'

'But not before the police arrive,' I told her firmly.

Tiny Bullen was at the gas cooker. With a box of matches in his hand, ready to light the gas under a kettle, he glanced round at me. 'Police!' he exclaimed.

'Yes, in the event of a sudden death they must always be called in.' I was repeating what I had said to Nurse Mackail and, looking at her, I added, 'I should like you to come back in here with me.' I made a movement indicating that she should go past me into the passage. For a moment I thought she was going to argue and I had no real authority to make her stay. But perhaps she was aware of the open-mouthed gaze of Tiny Bullen. At any rate she began to move back into the hall.

As I made to follow her my glance dropped to the floor. Here, in the kitchen, was an Indian rug which looked more suited to Tennant's quarters. In fact this rug was the only article that was *not* old in the Letts' part of the bungalow . . .

Mr Bullen tugged at my sleeve. 'Doctor — police, you said. It's not *murder*, is it?' he whispered.

I answered abruptly, 'That is a question you must ask the police when they arrive.' I daresay he saw he would get no further information out of me and hoped to have better luck with Nurse Mackail. At any rate he walked past me and on into the passage.

I looked again at the mat beneath my feet. I felt sure it had only recently been put there — though I did not remember seeing it in Tennant's part of the bungalow yesterday. But then, I had not been into his bedroom . . .

Suddenly I saw a glint of something white on the floor — close against the wall behind the door. The window was further along this same wall and, with the door shut, it was very dark in this corner. I stooped to look at what I took to be a scrap of paper, and instantly saw it was a small photo. I am sure at the time it did not occur to me that I ought not to have touched that piece of card, and I picked it up. A shock of surprise went through me as I looked at it. No . . . Oh, no . . .

And *then* I realized I was doing something wrong. I could hear footsteps outside and I knew the police were coming — but *this* was something they should not see. Deliberately I slipped the photo into my breast pocket.

I opened the door. I did not know Inspector Gore very well, though we had met on several occasions. Briefly now he greeted me with, 'Dr Jax — what is the trouble?'

With Gore was a sergeant, and the two of them followed me as I turned and led the way to the dead woman's room. In the hall stood Nurse Mackail and Tiny Bullen.

The Inspector was at my side as I advanced towards the bed, where I pulled back the sheet and silently pointed to the chief reason for his being called.

He asked quietly, 'Has she been dead long?'

'It's a bit difficult to say definitely,' I answered. 'Apparently the oven gas had been lit all night . . . That would keep the body temperature up . . . '

He looked at me and asked, 'Who found her?'

'Nurse Mackail,' I told him, and nodded towards the woman standing in the hall outside. She began to move into the room. She said, 'It was actually Mr Bullen who found Mrs Letts.'

'Very well — both of you come in,' Inspector Gore ordered. 'And you, Sergeant, but first go and ring up Sandy. Tell him I want him and Mearn here.'

When the sergeant returned he remained slightly behind Bullen and Nurse Mackail. I saw him take out his notebook.

The police inspector began to question the nurse, eliciting from her that she lived in Rook Lane, and had been fetched by Bullen. '*He* said he had come here to see if Mrs Letts was all right. He tried the door but couldn't open it.'

'Yes, that's right,' Tiny put in. 'At first I thought it was just the chain inside. Mrs

Letts had that on the door so that she could see who it was outside but didn't have to open the door unless it was someone she knew.'

'Go on,' Inspector Gore urged.

'Well I pushed but I knew it ought to open further than it did, even if the chain was on. Then I was sure there was something inside, so I went and fetched Nurse.'

'Why Nurse Mackail?'

Bullen seemed taken aback for a moment and a faint smile touched the nurse's lips. 'We *do* get fetched, like firemen, for all sorts of odd reasons,' she remarked.

'What happened when you got here?' the inspector asked.

'She was wedged against the door. We couldn't get in — so we called Charlie Herbert. I went out to the road to see if I could find help, and he was going by . . . '

'You say, 'She was wedged against the door.' What made you think it was Mrs Letts there?'

'We looked through the window — we could see a foot. Charlie forced the window and climbed in. He moved her enough to let us in . . . '

'You and Mr Bullen, you mean?'

'Yes.'

'Surely Charlie Herbert must have realised she was beyond help. Why didn't he get out of the window again and have us called?'

'Charlie! He's very slow . . . he couldn't have known. Anyway, *I* am not simple but I thought I could feel a flicker of her pulse . . . '

'When she had a blow like that on the back of her head?'

'I didn't know about that. It's very dark just inside the door . . . ' I could have corroborated that statement, but I said nothing. My glance lifted to the ceiling from the middle of which the electric light fitting, minus a bulb, hung on a dirty cord. Perhaps the nurse had seen my glance. She added, 'There is no electricity out in the kitchen, either — apparently they had to use candles.'

Inspector Gore said abruptly, 'That woman has been dead a good many hours — you should not have moved her. Why did you?' It was the same thing that I had asked her.

'I tell you. I thought there might be a chance of reviving her. I have known old folk to lie all night on the floor — cold as ice and half-dead from exposure — but got into bed, made warm with bottles and blankets — and they have lived.' The way she said it, quietly but firmly, carried conviction. *Could* she really have acted in good faith? I looked at her. She was a well-built young woman. She had capable-looking, spatulate fingered hands, large arms and broad shoulders.

I said, speaking for the first time since Gore began his questioning, 'It couldn't have been an easy decision for Nurse Mackail to make. Mrs Letts is heavy and it must have been *difficult* moving her.'

The nurse glanced at me and then away. She said, 'There were three of us — we managed.' And a nurse was trained to move dead weights, I reflected.

'You and Mr Bullen and Charlie Herbert,' the inspector said slowly. 'Where is Charlie now?'

'He left as soon as he had helped us, of

course. We didn't want *him* hanging round and hindering us.' That was Tiny Bullen.

'Hindering you? What did you have to do?'

'Why . . . well, Nurse rubbed her hands and I filled hot water bottles . . . ' As the man tugged at his moustache Inspector Gore was silent for a second or two. Then he asked, 'Why didn't *you* climb in through the window, Mr Bullen?'

'Me!' For a moment Tiny looked taken aback before he added, 'Can you imagine me scrambling in through windows? I would be too big and awkward . . . '

Gore gave Tiny a glance which travelled from his huge feet upwards to his shaggy untidy hair. After a short pause he questioned, 'Did the old woman live here alone?'

'No, she has a daughter and a lodger — Mr Tennant.' Again Bullen was the informant.

'Where are they now?' the inspector asked.

'I don't know. I saw them go off in his car last evening — about six or just before it would have been.'

'Tennant gives lectures,' I put in. 'I was here yesterday afternoon and he talked about going to Tonsford in the evening to give one.'

But Gore did not reply. He was looking at Nurse Mackail. 'You suggest that Mrs Letts could have been on the floor out there all night. Was she often left here alone?'

'I wouldn't know.'

'But I would,' put in Tiny. 'I don't ever remember it happening before. You see, I always hear the car come back. I'm only just opposite, you know, and they never bothered to be quiet. I'd hear them talking, banging doors and the like — but I didn't last night. That's partly why I came over this morning. Well, you never know — accidents happen these days, don't they? And I saw the car wasn't in the garage . . . '

As he spoke those words there came the sound of a car door slamming outside, and Nurse Mackail moved uneasily. 'I have several calls to make, Inspector. Can I go now?'

'I'm sorry — no,' came the quick reply. 'In fact I'm going to ask you and Mr Bullen to go down to the station.'

Tiny Bullen's hand had gone to his moustache, and tugging at it nervously he said sharply, '*I* haven't done anything. You can't put me in a cell . . . '

'I am not proposing to do that,' Gore told him. 'We just want your help in answering a few questions.'

The door opened and the two police-men came in — the reinforcements which had been sent for. Tiny Bullen looked at them. 'You want our *help*, eh? That's what you say when you pick up a murderer — but I tell you I'm not that. *I* haven't done anything.' He was gazing now at Gore, who said quietly, 'If you haven't done anything wrong there is nothing to be afraid of. Just tell the truth, that's all.'

The two were taken away and as the inspector left the bedroom I followed. I said, 'The nurse told the truth about having some cases to attend . . . '

He gave me a straight look. 'Oh . . . All right,' he said. 'I'll tell them to let her get on with her job — we can pick her up later today. Where is the phone?'

I opened the connecting door and as he stepped into Tennant's part he gave a low whistle. He used the telephone and then went on into the sitting room where only yesterday Mrs Letts had brought us sausages and hot rolls. I told him about my visit and Gore listened, looking around him. He said at last, 'It seems hardly possible that such luxury and squalor *could* be under the same roof.'

'No. I saw *this* part first,' I replied. 'It was a shock to me this morning to go into that sordid room at the back . . . ' I glanced from Inspector Gore to the sergeant standing just inside the door. I asked, 'All right if I go now?'

'Yes of course,' the inspector agreed at once. 'Naturally I'll need to contact you again.'

'You'll need me at the inquest,' I began.

'I'll see you before that,' he told me. 'I'll give you a ring.'

I had to go as I had come in — via the back way. Retracing my steps along the hall I glanced up at the heads on the wall.

They grinned down at me with seeming venom. I think yesterday, in Tennant's company and looking forward to good wine and refreshment, I had been impressed by these reminders of a hunter's adventures. Suddenly I disliked them very much, even though I could not say why. It was just a feeling of revulsion. Those *things* yesterday had been treated to an expensive toilet. Last night an old woman had died . . . alone . . . just along this passageway . . .

5

We found it impossible to get a maid to live in. Miss Turner, our daily woman, cooked a meal for us about five-thirty and then left. If there were no emergencies both Dad and I were free about that time, and Gwenda reached home just after five o'clock.

I was late that day as I had done most of my usual morning round during the afternoon. I was feeling tired and hungry. Dad was already at the table and Gwenda carrying in a pyrex dish when I got to the dining room. She put the dish on the table and lifted the lid. All day I had been unable to forget the happenings at The Elms that morning. All day I had wondered why Tennant and Madeline had not returned home last night — and whether the enquiries that must have been made had succeeded in locating them. Now, vividly, the aroma from that dish on our table reminded me of the moment when I had stepped into the Lett's kitchen — the warmth and the smell of cooking ... Somehow my appetite faded.

'Don't put me out too much,' I said.

Often lately our meals had been silent affairs and this evening was more quiet than usual.

Gwenda ladled vegetables and gravy on to our plates, and placed Dad's and mine in front of us. She sat down and we started eating, not because we knew we should enjoy the meal, but merely because it was there.

I glanced up. Dad was gazing abstractedly at his plate. He had eaten only a tiny portion of the heaped vegetables. Gwenda looked up too and her eyes met mine — for a brief second. And then she was looking at her plate again, stabbing anxiously at a roast potato. She was suddenly nervous.

I could sense it across the width of the table which separated us. Had I communicated my own distress to her in that quick glance? Did she know about that photograph — now in my wallet? I should have to ask her, but I could not do it here — with Dad at the table. I could not begin to talk about my morning's experience till I had my sister alone.

The telephone shrilled into my thoughts and I got up from my place, almost upsetting my chair as I did so. I knew, before I lifted the receiver, it was Inspector Gore on the other end of the wire. He said, 'I want to see you tonight. Can I come round to your home?'

'Yes, yes — of course. Are there any — developments?'

He didn't answer that question. Instead he told me, 'Also I want a word with Miss Jax. Will she be in?'

I was glad he could not see my face at that moment, for I might have betrayed more than the feigned surprise which I showed in my voice as I answered, 'My sister — why?'

'Can't tell you why, but I'd like her to be there. See you later. Goodbye, Doctor.' He rang off before I had a chance to ask him if there was any news of Madeline or Tennant.

Even after I had heard his handset click

back on to its cradle, I remained holding mine. At last I replaced it very slowly and as I moved away I was terribly aware of the photograph I had picked up that morning. Its possession was comfortable as itching powder against my skin would have been. Was the fact that Gore wanted to interview Gwenda anything to do with the picture I had found?

I heard the rattle of china and Gwenda began to cross the hall carrying a tray piled high with crocks.

'I'm going to make some coffee,' she said. 'Dad has gone into the sitting room.'

I moved towards her.

'Gwenda, there is something I want to tell you,' I said, and followed her into the kitchen. I waited till she had put the tray down.

'Mrs Letts has died . . . '

I was watching my sister's face, but it showed nothing — not surprise — or shock. I said, 'I thought you might have heard about it, but you didn't know . . . '

'Of course not,' Gwenda broke in. 'Why didn't you tell me when — well, when you first came in?'

I said slowly, 'I didn't really want to tell you at all — certainly not in front of Dad.' I was thinking of the death of our own mother.

'Mrs Letts was — murdered,' I added quietly.

Gwenda repeated my last word but she did not look at me. Pulling out the photograph I had found I said, 'Look at this.'

She put out her hand. 'Give me that,' she said hoarsely.

'No. I want to know about it. It is a wedding photograph . . . '

'Give it to me,' she repeated. She still refused to tell me anything, but that small print had told me a lot. I urged, 'Gwenda, can't you trust me? Inspector Gore is coming here this evening. He wants to see you.'

'Why?' Her eyes in her small face were wide. She reached again for the photograph. 'You won't show him that! Oh, Ian, burn it — please burn it. Not only for my sake I ask that.'

I said quietly, clearly, 'Gwenda, I'm going to tell you where I found this

— just where Mrs Letts had fallen — it must have been under her body . . . '

'Oh . . . ' My sister put both hands to her face.

'Can't you see? I had no *right* to bring this away. I did it for you . . . '

'Then destroy it,' she insisted.

I don't know why I did not accede to her pleadings. I must have seemed cruel to her. But I could not bring myself to do it. Perhaps I had the feeling that we might both be in a spot if we destroyed evidence . . . I don't know — but I replaced the photo in my breast pocket. I didn't know the man in it, but his face *was* familiar . . .

Her voice was low as she asked, 'Ian, do you want to *kill* me?'

For a moment I was shocked by the intensity of the word 'kill'. I said, 'Gwenda, I'll stand by you — no matter what. But if you won't give me your confidence, how can I really help?'

The doorbell rang and she moved quickly across the room. I saw her pull back her shoulders. I am sure she thought it was Gore, and she was nerving herself to face him. But only a moment later she returned to say in a brittle tone, 'It's Madeline Letts. Shall I show her into the waiting room?'

'No, I'll come,' I answered.

Madeline was in the hall. I beckoned her towards the dining room and held the door open for her to pass me. I expected Gwenda to come in as well but instead she turned back to the kitchen. I supposed she was going to make that coffee.

As soon as she reached me Madeline demanded, 'Where is my mother?' I admit I was nonplussed.

'Don't you know — anything?' I asked.

'No — except that the police are outside our bungalow. And we met Mr Bullen — on the corner of our road. He says they took my mother away on a stretcher.' Her face was strained and anxious. 'He told me it was perhaps best if I came to you. Tell me what's happened.'

'You say there are police outside The Elms. Why have you not asked *them*?'

'I was — scared. Wouldn't you be?'

'I don't think so. I always regard the police as my friends.' But did I? When I was determined, if possible, not to let them see what was in my pocket?

'Stop trying to put me off. Tell me where my mother is.' Madeline almost shouted at me.

But it was not my job to tell her that Mrs Letts had been murdered. It was not up to me to tell her anything. Yet I was a doctor. Perhaps I could lessen the shock for her . . .

I put a chair behind her. 'Sit down,' I commanded.

'No, no . . . '

'Well, your mother fell down — during the night probably — although she was not found until this morning. She has — died.'

'Oh . . . Oh . . . ' She sat down abruptly then.

But she did not react as a good many girls would by bursting into tears. After a moment she asked unexpectedly, 'Did she suffer?'

I said the kindest thing I could. 'Not for long I should think . . . But you will have to see the police, Madeline. There is nothing at all to be scared of.'

She stood up. 'If there is anything I can do to be of help I will,' I promised.

'Thank you — but . . . ' Another peal on the doorbell interrupted her. This would be the inspector. I waited, expecting Gwenda would go to let him in, but again the bell rang and I went myself into the hall. There was no sign of my sister. I opened the door. In the porch was Inspector Gore. Ralph Tennant was beside him. Gore said, 'Miss Letts is here, I believe?' I nodded.

'Mind if we both come in?' came the demand.

'No.' I led the way to the dining room and let the two men in. Then I turned and went to the kitchen. If Gwenda had the coffee nearly ready it might be a good idea if we all had some. Certainly a hot strong drink might help Madeline. But there was no welcome aroma in the kitchen, and Gwenda was not there. Back in the hall, I glanced towards the stand where her coat always hung when she was in. It was not there. She must have gone out after Madeline arrived. To avoid the inspector?

I returned to the dining room. Madeline was in a chair with Ralph Tennant standing beside her, his arm round her shoulder. She was not relaxed against him but sat bolt upright, her gaze fixed on the inspector, who was saying, 'You were not there all night. Where were you?'

'I . . . we went . . . Ralph and I — to give a lecture at Tonsford.'

'I know that — but you did not come back. Apparently you have only just returned.'

'Yes, Ralph had heard of a short cut and we decided to try it coming home.'

Gore's glance went to Tennant who said, '*Try* it is right. The fool who told me to go that way must have been a practical joker. We got bogged down and I went to get help. I walked miles . . . '

'I thought he was *never* coming back,' Madeline put in. 'When he did — with a breakdown lorry, it took ages to haul us out *and* we had a broken something . . . '

Tennant said, 'Yes, the back axle. We had to have it repaired. They towed us back to Tonsford . . . '

Suddenly Madeline stood up. 'And then I come home — to — this,' she said, looking at Gorc. 'Can't I go home now?'

'Yes,' he agreed. Her face was pale and drawn.

'I'm sorry about it all,' I said. 'Look, I'll go into surgery and get you something . . . '

'I don't believe in drugs and the like,' she interrupted as she started to move towards the door. 'There will be a lot to be done and I don't want to be dazed with sedatives.'

I felt a quick surge of admiration for her. 'At least have a glass of sherry,' I urged.

'No. No, thank you.' Her head, with its pile of blonde hair was held high, her step firm. I opened the door for her, went along the hall and let her out. Ralph Tennant followed her.

I heard the slam of a car door, the starting of the engine. When I knew they had gone I went slowly back towards the dining room. I would have now to confess to the inspector that Gwenda had gone out. Dash it all — why had I shown her that wretched photo before he came? If she hadn't known it was in my possession she could have given nothing away . . .

Yet she had never been the sort to funk consequences. Surely she must know that she would be letting me down if she didn't see Gore. I had told him she would be here . . .

I had my hand out to push open the dining room door when she came out of the kitchen. She was wearing her coat, but I did not ask her where she had been. I said, 'Inspector Gore is waiting to see you.'

I watched her as she crossed the hall. Her hands trembled as she hung her coat on its peg, but as she passed me to enter the dining room she looked perfectly self-possessed.

Yet as we got inside it was not to her that the inspector spoke first. Looking at me, he remarked, 'It would appear more natural for Miss Letts to go home first — yet she came here.'

'As a matter of fact she did go to The Elms — but spotted one of your men outside. For some reason she was scared and decided not to try to go in.'

'But why come to *you?*'

'She met Mr Bullen — whether by design or accident when it concerns that old busybody, it would be difficult to guess. Anyway, he advised Madeline to come to me. I can't imagine why he didn't spill the whole box of tricks right away. But quite obviously he had told her nothing.'

'Glad to know he is obeying orders,' the inspector returned drily. 'I told him in no uncertain terms *not* to gossip to anyone.'

His glance swerved abruptly in Gwenda's direction. 'I'd like to know why you went to the Letts' bungalow last evening — about six-thirty-five,' he said.

'Who told you I went there?' my sister demanded, but Gore did not reply at once and Gwenda said, her voice firm, 'I did not go *near* Rook Lane last night.'

'That was all I wanted to ask you,' came the quiet reply as the inspector began to move across the room.

Gwenda turned abruptly and went ahead of him out through the doorway. I was aware that she had deliberately avoided my glance, and very acutely I was conscious of the secret between us — that photo. I had been tensed, feeling somehow that Gore might have known about it. Yet how could he — or *anyone* know that I had it?

But I had to admit to myself that I was worried. The photo that I had found . . . Now this suggestive question as to why Gwenda had gone to the Letts' bungalow last evening . . . added to the fact that I could not ask her about that — not after she had been so obviously determined not to give me her confidence . . .

After I had let the inspector out I felt I did not want to go back and see Gwenda. I opened the door of the study and, going across to the desk, sat down. But I did not attempt to do any work. I sat elbows on desk, chin in hands, gazing down at the polished top.

And for apparently no reason at all I found I was remembering the rice pudding Gwenda had served up as dessert.

'Old rice pudding . . . ' The three words ran insistently through my mind. I took a small memo book from a drawer, looked up a number, and reached for the telephone.

6

Bill Rice arrived the next day. He had been at the university with me, and at irregular intervals ever since we had come into touch with one another. I knew his father was pretty well-off and had decided Bill should go into big business and be a company director.

But my friend had other ideas. He was not at all the stodgy rice pudding indicated by our nickname for him. He had dabbled in all sorts of projects — some of which had taken him to widely scattered parts of the globe. He had met many people, criminals among them, before he eventually made up his mind to become a private detective.

Up to now he had successfully solved a dozen or more puzzling cases. I was remembering this fact as I faced him across the desk in my study. Our preliminary greetings were over and now he was saying, 'Start at the beginning

— and don't omit anything, even if you imagine it to be trivial.'

So I told him about my vague worry over Gwenda, my mother's suicide and Dad's reaction to the tragedy — my conviction that something more than mother's death was troubling him.

I got to the murder of Mrs Letts. 'That is really why I have asked you to come,' I told him, and related about the way Inspector Gore had come here yesterday. 'Mostly to ask Gwenda why *she* went to the Letts' bungalow on the evening of the murder. She denies the allegation. Of course I don't know who said she had been there — or if she really did go. To ask her would be to admit I think she could have been lying . . . '

'Was she?' Bill shot the question at me, and I hesitated.

'I know her pretty well,' I admitted at last. 'Somehow I don't believe she was telling the truth. What worries me is that the inspector may think the same.'

'And, like you, will be wondering what she is trying to hide. Have *you* any idea?'

'No.'

'Well, put me a bit more in the picture about the woman who was murdered,' Bill said.

I described Mrs Letts and the bungalow, recently let in part to Tennant.

I remarked, 'Ralph Tennant must be well-off with all the luxury he displays. He surely earns a good bit with the lectures he gives all over the place, but he can't have paid his landlady much — or she would have lived in a little more comfort herself.'

'Not necessarily. She could have some salted away in a stocking. It isn't always those who *appear* most poor who are.'

'If she did have money hidden in her room the murder motive could have been robbery,' I suggested.

'*Could* have,' he agreed. 'On the other hand we don't know — not till we know how much — or how little — she had.' My friend spoke slowly. 'We will have to try and find that out.'

'Even Madeline, her daughter, might be unaware of all the mother owned.'

'Just so.' Bill stroked one finger across

his eyebrow in a mannerism I remembered well. He was silent for quite a while before he added, 'Tell me about this Madeline — and I want every tiny detail of what happened when you were called to the bungalow that morning.'

I related the occurrence as clearly as I could. He did not interrupt till I came to Nurse Mackail.

Then he asked, 'I can hardly take it in that a trained nurse really believed the woman to be alive. How about you, Ian?'

'*If* she did, then she was right to get Mrs Letts into a warm bed. And of course there would be no sign of bleeding from the injuries by next morning. I have been thinking a lot about that since. Why was there so little sign of blood — no more than you would expect from a small wound like the one on her forehead?'

Bill gave a small non-committal grunt. I said after a moment or two, 'It couldn't have been a stranger who killed Mrs Letts — for robbery or any other motive.'

'How have you worked that out?'

'She kept a chain on her back door — she would not have let in anyone she did not know. And she was found wedged against that door — so nobody could have gone out that way. Whoever did it let himself out by the front way, taking the key with him . . . '

'Or *her*,' Bill interposed.

'You don't really think a *woman* could have done a brutal murder like that?' I asked, and knew that fear was gripping my heart. In some way my own sister was involved in this affair . . . which *I* had asked Bill to come and try to unravel.

I said, 'I suppose Madeline Letts had a key.'

'But how far does that get us?' he demanded. 'You say it was a Mr Bullen who gave the information that there was always a spare key left on the narrow ledge just inside the front door. Whoever left the bungalow last probably took that key, used it and, possibly, threw it away. I wonder if the police have tried to find it.'

'If they have I should imagine it was pretty unlikely it would turn up,' I answered. 'A door key is a very small item.'

'You'd be surprised what tiny articles

can come to light sometimes,' Bill retorted. 'A clue smaller even than a key has been known to result in the conviction of a criminal.' He stood up.

'I think I'll go along and book in at your local hotel,' he said. 'No, no, don't offer to put me up here. I'd rather be a free agent — to go in and out when and as I like.'

7

When I got downstairs that morning Gwenda had already had her breakfast. As soon as I appeared in the dining room doorway she said, 'I'm off.'

'You are going early,' I remarked.

'I have to do overtime occasionally,' she replied, and dashed past me to put on her coat. As I stood watching her go I noticed that the newspapers were pushed through the letter box, and I followed my sister along the hall to fetch them. Usually she got them and put them on the table with our mail.

As I returned to the dining room I wished we could get back to our old happy life — but could we ever? Dad was a changed man. Gwenda, who had once been a gay companion, was now aloof and reserved — even more so since the evening following the death of Mrs Letts . . .

Gwenda had always been small. Now

her face seemed even tinier than ever, perhaps because it was never plumped by merriment. I used to tease her and say she looked as though she was blowing up a balloon when she laughed. She didn't even smile now. And I found it impossible to try teasing her.

And Mother — the dear queen-pin of all our lives — she left a gap which could never be filled — and an incomprehensible mystery. I still could not understand why my gentle mother, with her resolute faith that everything was for the best in the best of all possible worlds, should have taken her own life.

Dad rarely now put in an appearance at breakfast so alone I started on my solitary meal. This was the morning for the delivery of our local weekly, and as I unfolded it from inside the daily, I caught the heading right across the top of its front page. 'Murder. Old lady attacked — left to die.'

The words seemed almost to hit me, for there were never headlines like that on my own staid newspaper. That was concerned with politics and the international situation, while murders were reported only briefly on an inside page. But of course the Mewsdale weekly was making the most of the local tragedy.

My eyes glanced quickly over the closely printed type. The inquest jury had brought in a verdict of murder against a person or persons unknown. It was now up to the police to discover who the 'person or persons unknown' were.

I finished my breakfast and went along the passage to the study, where I guessed I should find my secretary already busy. She smiled at me. 'I guess you heard the phone ring not long ago,' she said and I nodded.

'Anything urgent?' I asked.

'Miss Letts is ill — at The Elms.'

I sensed that she was looking at me curiously. She, too, had probably read that newspaper report — knew that I had been at Madeline's home on the afternoon before Mrs Letts died. But I was not prepared to make any comment.

I asked, 'Did they say what was the matter with Miss Letts?'

'No, it was a rather vague message. I couldn't get much sense out of the caller. But naturally that poor girl would be upset. Perhaps she is in for a breakdown.' But I hardly heard the last part of Mrs Watson's speech. As I turned away I was remembering Gwenda and the way she had rushed off early to business. The newspapers had been still in the letter box, yet she *had* seen that report. Quite surely she had taken out the bundle and then put it back. Gwenda had not wanted to discuss what was splashed across that front page.

I had been to the inquest yesterday but Gwenda had gone straight on from her office to the theatre with a friend, and I had not seen her last evening. This morning she had given me no chance to tell her anything — but she *knew* the verdict. Before I came downstairs she had read that report for herself.

★　★　★

When I got out to start my round I decided to go first to The Elms. I knocked at the front door, thinking that perhaps Tennant would let me in, but there was no reply and I decided to go to the back.

When I turned the angle of the bungalow I was faced with the door I remembered very well. On my left was a window and as I walked past this it was quietly opened. A key was thrust towards me. Madeline's voice whispered, 'That unlocks the back door. Come on in and fasten it behind you.'

She was in a bed under the window — and in a room opposite the one where not many days before I had gone to see her mother . . .

The blonde hair, straggling round her shoulders, had lost its sheen and was showing dark at the roots. Her face was flushed and she looked distressed. I put one hand on her forehead, the other on her pulse. In the same instant there were sounds of movement outside — a loud knock on the door. Madeline pulled up her bedclothes, almost hiding her face. 'It's the police,' she whispered. 'Don't let them come in. I won't . . . I can't talk to them.'

I was certain she was in no fit state to be interviewed. I went to the door and told Gore so. Through the window I, like Madeline, had seen who was there. He said, 'Actually it's Tennant as well as the girl I want to see. Find out if he's in. If he *is* he won't answer the door at the front. I rang the bell just now.'

I went back to Madeline. 'It's all right,' I told her. 'The police are human, you know. No one shall worry you till you are better.'

She said, 'Ralph has left here — he says he can't stay — not now I'm on my own. But that's when I want someone. With all these trees round the bungalow it's eerie.'

'But you've always lived here,' I remarked.

'I know — but it's different when you are all alone. I keep hearing noises and I keep wishing . . . ' She shuddered, turned and buried her face in the pillow.

'Where *is* Tennant?' I asked.

'Staying at the hotel. He said he'd come and see me yesterday but he hasn't been — nor this morning . . . ' Her voice was distraught.

I gave her an injection and said I'd find a woman to come and stay with her till she was well again and could decide whether she wanted to stay on at The Elms or not. 'I'll lock you in and take the key with me,' I said. 'Then if you have gone to sleep the person I send can let herself in without disturbing you. I'll get someone just as soon as possible.'

'You're a good sort, Ian.' She clung to my hand. 'You won't let those policemen come near me, will you?'

'Not until you are *able* to see them,' I promised.

When I got outside Bill was there, on the corner, obviously waiting for me. As we walked along by the side of the bungalow I told him what Madeline had said about Tennant.

'So this Tennant is a gentleman,' Bill remarked. 'He won't compromise the girl by staying there now her mother is gone. I was hoping I'd be able to meet him. I'll go back to the hotel presently and see if I can locate him. I have a sudden wonder as to whether I shall find him.'

'I'm sure you will,' I replied. 'I like Ralph.'

'I'm disappointed I shall not be able to talk to Madeline Letts. I was not visible — but I heard what you said to the inspector . . . ' He grinned at me, and then added, 'But you told me Tiny Bullen lived opposite here. Can you spare the time to take me in to see him?'

'I haven't any very serious case on my list,' I told him, 'so I can give you about twenty minutes.'

I led the way across the road and along Tiny's garden path. The door was opened almost before I reached it and Bullen said, 'I saw you on the way in. Come along, Doctor — nice to see you.'

'I have brought my friend with me. Do you mind if he comes in as well?' I asked. 'He is a detective.'

A small dog barked furiously as we went into the hall and Tiny called, 'Rocket, come here.' He was leading the way into his sitting room where he waved us towards a couple of armchairs. I said, 'Mr Rice is interested in our murder case. Can you tell him who was in Mr

Tennant's car when it left on Thursday evening?'

'Him and Madeline.'

'You saw them get in? You are *sure* it was Miss Letts and Mr Tennant? Think before you reply,' Bill said.

'Yes, they came out of the front door and across to the car, like they always did.'

'Just the two of them?'

'Yes.'

'Who was driving?' Bill asked.

'Him of course — he always did.'

'But Miss Letts could drive. Are you sure *she* did not get into the driving seat? You do know she could drive?'

'I never saw her,' Tiny asserted. 'Now listen — the car was facing me — so the wheel would be on my left . . . '

'Yes,' Bill agreed, standing up and going to the window. 'Come here and tell me just where the car was standing.'

Tiny described exactly where Tennant's Singer was always left.

'And what was the time?' Bill asked. 'I mean when they drove away.'

'It must have been just before six. I

know I'd heard the clock chime the quarter to, and I was thinking it was nearly time for them to go. He was giving a series of lectures at Tonsford and they'd been leaving about that time on a Thursday for the last few weeks.'

Bill stood silently looking out of the window for some moments before he asked, 'What happened next — after they had gone?'

'I went over to see Mrs Letts.'

'Straightaway?'

'As good as. I had to stop to put on a jacket. Well, she was glad of company sometimes and that's why I used to pop over there. But she didn't seem to want me to stop that night. She was putting something in a casserole. 'For them when they come back,' I said to her. 'Don't know why you bother when they treat you like dirt.' And she rounded on me — told me to mind my own business. Well, I was only sticking up for her, but it put her in a right huffy mood. Mind you, she could be like that at times — best to leave her alone when she was in that kind of temper, I'd found. So I came back home.

She usually gave me a cup of tea, but I didn't get one that evening.' It sounded as though he resented being cheated of his tea . . .

He added, 'I don't know why she should have been so touchy about *them* — she wasn't usually. That Tennant fellow — well, I ask you, Madeline's his unpaid assistant that's what she is . . . '

As he paused Bill suggested, 'You don't like Mr Tennant.' Tiny gave him a quizzical look and then said hastily, 'I didn't say that.'

'No — all right. Now, you were apparently not welcome at The Elms and did not stay. What happened next?'

Bill gave me a quick glance and then returned his attention to Bullen who was saying, 'I saw the Doctor's sister go in not long after I left there myself.' The man looked at me uncertainly, but Bill urged, 'Go on — tell me exactly what you saw — and I'm not forgetting that at this time of the evening it must have been nearly dark. How can you be sure it was Dr Jax's sister you saw?'

Tiny was looking at me now. 'You sure

it's all right for me to be telling this?' he demanded. I did not know whether he meant on my behalf, or if he was remembering that Inspector Gore had told him not to gossip to *anyone*. But somehow Gwenda was mixed up in all this — and Bill needed to know the facts.

'You carry on,' I assured him. 'It's perfectly all right.'

'Well then . . . ' Bullen's gaze returned to Bill. 'I'd gone back indoors to fetch Rocket. You know — or perhaps you don't — how dark it is just inside my driveway with that thick holly arch over my gate. But there's a lamp opposite.' He pointed. Immediately in front of the Letts' bungalow was a street lamp.

'I saw this girl go quickly under that light and turn in at the gate of The Elms. I saw her plain as plain. I'd know Doctor's sister anywhere — with her fawn fluffy coat. Like a little Bambi she is — the way she trips along. And her hair down to her shoulders — with a band of red ribbon across it.'

That was Gwenda all right . . .

Bill left the window and returned to his chair.

'You saw her come out again?' Bill demanded. He was very much the detective now. I feel sure he had forgotten this was Gwenda being talked about. But *I* could not forget. Gwenda was my sister. I walked restlessly across to the window and back again.

Tiny said slowly, 'No, I didn't see her come out.' Then he added a trifle tartly, 'I don't have time to watch my neighbours' doings every minute of the day.'

But there was little that went on in the places around that he did *not* see . . .

Bill said placatingly, 'We — the police and private detectives like myself — have to rely on the general public to help us, you know. If they notice things that are a bit odd it may tell us more than they imagine sometimes. Windows open that are normally shut — someone prowling suspiciously round a place — lights . . . '

'Ah now,' Tiny broke in. 'I did notice there was a light on in the front room after Madeline and Mr Tennant had left. But then, they might have forgot it. I

104

know once it was on all night . . . '

'But that was most unusual? Mrs Letts wouldn't go into the sitting room to watch the T.V. or something like that . . . '

'Her! No, she couldn't abide having it in her place really. 'Noisy, unholy thing,' she called it. Madeline always wanted one. She triumphed when that lodger insisted on having his in.'

Madeline, siding with Tennant against her mother . . . That could have been some of the reason for Mrs Letts' hate . . .

'There is another thing,' I put in. 'I was there during the afternoon.'

'I know — I saw you go in. I did wonder if you'd left something behind and Miss Jax had come back to fetch it . . . '

That was an excuse Gwenda could have made to Gore the other night. Why hadn't she? Because, she said, she had not been here . . .

I went on with what I had been about to say when Tiny interrupted. 'There was another visitor over there at the same time as myself. Did you see *him* leave?' I looked at Bill. Perhaps he might not want my questioning — but he was gazing at Bullen who answered, 'No. Didn't see him *come* neither.'

Tiny might assert that he didn't closely watch his neighbours, but he was aggrieved that he had missed seeing *anyone* go into The Elms. 'What was he like?' came the demand.

'That's immaterial if you didn't see him,' I began, and Tiny looked at me crossly.

'I *might* have seen him, mightn't I? When I took Rocket out I might have seen him, but how would I be able to say if I didn't know what he was like?'

'You'd know if you saw a stranger near here,' Bill put in.

'Ah yes. Now I always go the same way — along our road, then up Pines Cutting and back past the church, so I've been all the way round. And I did meet someone that night — a man. He had a cap pulled down over his eyes and he turned into the Cutting as I was getting to the end of it. But he stopped short, turned round and went back. He didn't want me to see him.

And he *could* have been going to The Elms, couldn't he?'

Bill stood up. 'I'll remember what you've told me, but you didn't see him close to. You couldn't describe him.'

'No . . . '

'Well I can't imagine it's important. Anyway, thank you for answering my questions . . . '

Bill was moving out of the room now. I said goodbye to Tiny and then went too. I reached the gate just behind Bill. 'Because of *his* tale the inspector wanted to see Gwenda the other night. That old busy-body — you can't take all *he* says as gospel truth.'

'I know, Ian. But I'm an investigator. I have to sift all the evidence I am given — and sift it again. I have to discover whether I have been told the truth or an untruth — even if what folk *think* they have seen is actuality.' Bill gave me a quick look.

'Ian, this is spoken as a friend. *If* your sister came here that evening, then it would be best if she admitted it.'

I felt a small thrust of anger. 'Bill, it's

only Tiny Bullen's word against Gwenda's. I know who *I* would trust most.'

'Of course — I understand,' Bill said and moved towards his car. 'But talk to Gwenda — as a brother . . . '

I began to cross the road. I reached the Consul. As I slammed the door and started up I was remembering my own reaction to Tiny's description of the girl he saw that evening — so vivid, so unmistakable. I had thought, 'that's Gwenda all right.'

Tiny had known us since we were children. He wouldn't want to do either of us a bad turn. He had been fond of Gwenda — liking to chuck her under the chin . . . My thoughts pulled up short as I remembered Gwenda talking about that. Had Tiny felt — and resented — her recoil? But he wouldn't, he couldn't be mean enough to try and harm her in this way . . .

I turned out of Rook Lane and drove straight home. My daily woman was busy in the hall with her Hoover. I motioned her to switch it off and then said quickly, 'Do you know anyone who would go and stay with Miss Letts for a day or so? The girl is ill — needs a woman there all the time for a little while.'

'Stay in *that* place at *night?*' Miss Turner demanded.

'There is nothing at The Elms to hurt anyone,' I answered quietly. 'I was relying on you to help me. I thought you would surely know of someone and . . . '

She switched on the Hoover and pushed it across the carpet in a crescendo of noise that effectively drowned what I had been about to say. I felt annoyed by the rude interruption, but impotent to do anything about it. Domestic workers were hard to come by and we were lucky to have someone who came regularly and did her work well. Her manners I had no power to control. I began to turn away.

Then the noise of the machine whirred into silence and she said, 'You could try Sarah Yeats. She lives next door to me and hasn't got no job at the moment. Don't say I recommended her, though — because I don't. I doubt, anyway, she'll go to The Elms — any more than *I* would.'

But the woman did agree to accompany me — 'just for the day.' As our own daily had said, there was some sort of superstitious fear attached to staying all night in a place where a murder had been committed. I promised I would fetch Mrs Yeats away myself that evening — yet I knew I *must* find someone else for the night.

I could spare no time now, however. Other cases were awaiting my visits. Well, perhaps during the day I should discover someone if I kept the matter in mind . . .

As though for very long at a time I should be *able* to forget the Letts affair. I was involved in it. My sister was involved in it. *Bill* believed Gwenda had visited The Elms that night — and I would have to tackle her about it. There would be no chance till this evening and it was a task I did not look forward to . . .

I was late in to my lunch. When I should have been finishing it I was only just beginning — and as I picked up my knife and fork the phone rang. I heard

Miss Turner leave the kitchen to answer it. A moment later she put her head in at the door to say, 'It's for you — personal, he said.'

Reluctantly I got up. Some of these 'personal' calls were only patients or their relatives determined to contact 'the fountain-head' as one man had once put it to me. Why hadn't I told Miss Turner to say I was out and a message must be left? Anyway, she wasn't always willing to co-operate . . .

I picked up the receiver and gave my name.

'Oh, Ian . . . Bill here. You know who — he was *not* there when I got back this morning.' He did not intend to mention Tennant's name over the phone.

'Oh! You mean he has left the hotel? Not for good?'

'He hasn't paid his bill but he has taken his case with him. Still, I'll pick up his trail, I've no doubt.'

But Tennant was not a suspect. He had been miles away with Madeline long before Mrs Letts had died.

Late that afternoon I had still not

found anyone to stay the night at The Elms and I was on my way in the forlorn hope that Charlie Herbert's mother would agree to go. Charlie had climbed in through the window and helped to move Mrs Letts. He was hefty but he had more brawn than brain. His mother, too, was none too bright — but perhaps someone like that would lack the imagination of these other superstitious women . . .

The sight of a figure ahead of me interrupted my thoughts and made me pull to a halt after a few more yards. Opening the door of my car I asked, 'Want a lift, Tennant?'

He looked round at me and then, beginning to get in, said, 'I'm going to the station.'

'Going away, you mean?'

'No — to meet someone. Is it on your way?'

'I'm going right by it,' I said and then added as I let in the clutch, 'I went to see Madeline this morning — she is rather ill. Did you know?'

'Yes — I've just come from the bungalow — but she was asleep.'

'She told me *you* were staying at the Lion.'

'For a night or so.'

Why didn't I tell him that Bill had gone there looking for him? But I did not. Instead I said, 'Madeline is suffering partly from delayed shock.'

'Yes? I know she didn't appear to be upset when the old girl died but then, there was never any love lost between those two — or at least that's the way it struck me. Of course I haven't been here all that long . . . '

'Mrs Letts did a lot for Madeline, I believe — and any girl is bound to be upset when her mother dies. That is obviously showing in Madeline's case now. I don't think she will want to go on living at The Elms.'

'Why ever not?' he broke in. Remembering what Miss Turner's reaction had been *and* that of Sarah Yeats, I thought there was really no need for him to ask that. If those women did not like the idea of being in the bungalow, how about Madeline who was so very closely implicated?

Tennant was going on to say, 'That's her home — and now we can have *all* the bungalow.'

'You mean you and she will — marry?' I asked.

There was a long pause. Of course I'd had no right to ask that, and perhaps he would tell me to mind my own business. He did not. He shrugged. 'Maybe,' he admitted.

I turned the Consul into the station approach. He was adding, 'In the meantime we must have someone to do for us. I have found a woman who will live in. That's who I am meeting at the station.'

This was a relief to me. *Now* I had no need to go and see Mrs Herbert. I told him what I had been intending to do.

'You have solved my problem for me,' I said, 'for I couldn't have left Madeline alone there all night. Look, I have promised to fetch Mrs Yeats away from The Elms, so if you like I'll wait for you . . .'

'And taxi Mrs Hodgson round there on your way?' Tennant put in. 'That's very decent of you, Jax.'

The train came in only a few moments after we arrived. Tennant went on to the platform to meet his visitor and I watched them come through the barrier. Just ahead of him, she carried a small case and a handbag. Tennant was hefting an obviously weighty large suitcase. It looked as though Mrs Hodgson had come to stay . . .

When they reached me he introduced us and she murmured, 'How do you do?' But she did not look up at me. I opened the back door of the car for her and she got in. Sitting down, she settled into a corner, her gaze fixed on the bag which she held clutched in her lap.

She did not speak during the whole of our drive to The Elms. She did not seem to hear when I remarked that I hoped she would like Mewsdale. Was she reserved — or taciturn? When I helped her out I looked at her. She was dark-skinned, with a chin that was pointed, and a long thin nose. I found myself studying the bones of her sharp face — partly because I was a doctor — partly because she was so thin. I guessed her eyes would be dark to match that brown skin, but I did not *know* — for still she did not look at me.

I went in to see Madeline. The girl was restless, tossing uneasily and muttering through dry lips. Mrs Yeats said she had roused not long before and had a cup of tea, but refused anything to eat.

I put my hand on Madeline's wrist and, bending over, spoke her name. Her eyes opened. 'Don't let them come,' she whispered, and I supposed she was still worried about the police's visit. 'Ian, I heard . . . I heard . . . ' Her voice trailed away.

'What did you hear?' I asked.

Her voice was hoarse. 'I heard her moaning . . . moaning . . . ' She started up convulsively 'Don't leave me alone,' she begged.

'I won't,' I promised.

I gave her an injection. Madeline might not believe in drugs, but had to have them now. Mrs Yeats was hovering in the doorway.

'Where is Mr Tennant?' I asked, and she motioned to the door connecting the back with the front part of the bungalow. As I opened the door I could hear voices but immediately they stopped. I went along to the sitting room and, tapping on the panel, called, 'Tennant?'

'Come in,' he replied.

He was there with the newly arrived Mrs Hodgson. I said, 'I'm a trifle worried about Madeline. If she should get any worse in the night I am to be called.'

'Yes — all right,' Tennant answered. 'But if it's only delayed shock there is no danger, is there?'

I told him, 'I'm not sure it is only that.' I moved nearer to the woman and spoke clearly, 'Mrs Hodgson, you will be in charge of Miss Letts. You do understand that I must be called should there be any change in her condition.'

'Of course she understands,' Tennant put in quickly. 'Mrs Hodgson had experience when she nursed her husband . . . ' And then for the first time I saw the woman look up — yet even then I did not see the colour of her eyes, nor the expression in them — they were so very deep-set. She had glanced at Tennant.

Now she began to move with a shuffling gait across the room.

'If this girl is dying I'd better go to her,' she said, and her voice was like a reed instrument from the east — mysterious and somehow sinister. I barred her way. I said, 'Miss Letts is *not* dying. If . . . if anything *does* happen to her then I'll want to know *why*, but the folk in this house will have to account to a higher authority than me.' I did not know what had made me say that, but suddenly I felt worried at the thought of leaving Madeline to this hag's care.

The woman began to push past me and I let her go. As I heard her retreating along the hall I said, 'Tennant, I don't know where you found her, but I don't like her.'

'As you made quite clear.' He laughed. 'A bungling coroner's jury brings in a verdict of murder on an old woman, and everyone seems to become melodramatic,' he said. 'It's not a role that really suits you, though, Jax. Mrs Hodgson might not be the one I would select myself — but I can't afford to be choosey.

This is my home now. I have all my things around me here. But I'm no good at looking after myself — not when I don't have to. I loathe cooking. That's a woman's job — so get a woman to do it, I say. Besides, there is Madeline. She needs a bit of nursing and, on your own admission, you were finding it difficult to get anyone to come here.'

'Yes. So how did you do it?' I asked.

'Went to a different town naturally,' he replied.

'And so *she* knows nothing about what happened to Mrs Letts?'

'If I have my way she won't find out, either,' he said.

But he still hadn't explained just how he came to get in touch with the woman . . . I was thinking that as I turned to go out of the room. Here was someone who was coming in almost at once to take Mrs Letts' place — someone who could, possibly, have had an interest in getting rid of Madeline's mother . . . It might be worth looking into this woman's past — but that was Bill's job. I was not the detective.

As I put my hand on the door handle Tennant laughed again. 'The one in the kitchen doesn't need to be an oil painting, does she? It is the woman you spend your leisure with who needs the looks . . . '

Madeline, for instance, I thought as I made my way back to the kitchen. But Madeline was no picture of delight at the moment, ill as she was.

Mrs Hodgson was at the sink, filling a kettle. Mrs Yeats already had on her hat and coat. 'Come on, Doctor,' she called. 'Let's get out of here.'

In the car she said, 'The police came this afternoon. I let them in — was that all right?'

'I told you no one was to disturb Miss Letts.'

'Oh they didn't — she was asleep. They went in the other rooms — was that all right?'

'Yes,' I told her. Gore had a job to do, the same as I had, and if he wanted to look over the bungalow again, that was his business.

★ ★ ★

That evening when surgery was over and our supper finished Dad went off as usual to the sitting room. Gwenda piled a tray with crocks and I said, 'I'll carry that out to the kitchen.'

'All right.' She picked up a plate of cakes in one hand, in the other a dish of sausage rolls which had not been touched. We had none of us, apparently, had much appetite.

I said, 'Wait a minute, Gwenda. Were you at the Letts' bungalow — the evening Madeline's mother died?'

She turned, moving a step or two towards the door. She did not intend to answer me. In a couple of strides I reached her, took the two plates from her. 'Why did you go there?' I demanded. For a moment it was as though she was frozen. Her arms remained extended in front of her. 'Gwenda, can't you trust me?'

Then her arms dropped limply to her sides. 'It sounds as though you don't trust *me*,' she said bitterly. 'I told you I did not

121

go there. You suggest that I am lying.' She swung away from me.

'Gwenda, I didn't want to say anything to you but . . . ' I told her about my visit to Tiny Bullen that morning. I wanted her to turn and face me. I wanted to be able to see her eyes — the clear, frank eyes which had loved to smile, yet now seemed to have forgotten how to conjure up that gaiety from within. But she remained with her back to me.

'Bullen says he saw you go into The Elms that night.'

'And you believe him before me? Inspector Gore believes *him*.'

I put the plates back on the table. I moved round to the front of her, put out my hands and held her gently by the shoulders.

I said, 'Look at me. Tell me the truth. I don't know why you seem all tensed-up lately. I don't know why you may have gone to The Elms — if you did. Unless you want to tell me, don't. I'm not curious, only . . . '

'No,' she broke in, that note of bitterness still in her voice. 'The inspector is curious and has persuaded you to do his dirty work for him.'

'You are quite wrong,' I retorted, and then paused, wondering if I should tell her about Bill. The police were an inevitable result of the murder — they necessarily came to ask questions — but she might resent it if she knew *I* had called in a private investigator — even though he was a friend.

'It's just that I love you,' I told her. 'I'd give my right hand to help you out of any trouble.' I saw the way her lip trembled and for a moment thought I had broken her resistance. Then abruptly she turned out of my hold. 'Thank you, but I haven't anything to tell you,' she said.

★ ★ ★

I went the next morning to see Madeline Letts. She was slightly better, but still ill. Mrs Hodgson went with me into the bedroom and followed me when I left. I gave her some instructions about treatment for the patient. She was unnervingly impassive and silent. I wondered if she had heard what I had said, and I began to repeat my directions in a louder voice.

She said in that reedy voice, 'I'm not deaf.'

'Oh . . . Well can I see Mr Tennant?'

She nodded her head towards the connecting door, and I went along the passage. In the hall I could not resist a glance up at the fiercely grinning alligators, but I had taken only a few steps before a head was poked out of the sitting room doorway. I exclaimed, 'Bill!' I went on and into the room.

'The inspector is here as well,' Bill told me. 'I have introduced myself.'

I thought that Inspector Gore's nod to me lacked any cordiality. I said, 'I wondered if I'd find Mr Tennant here.'

'No, he's gone off on some business for the day.'

'You haven't made an arrest yet,' I ventured.

'No.'

My glance had gone to the corner where Tennant's collection of sticks had been. They were all missing. I said with

124

conviction, 'One of *those* was the murder weapon.'

The inspector glanced at me and then asked, 'Any objections to letting me have a set of your fingerprints?'

'No of course not,' I answered, 'and I can tell you now that if you are testing those sticks for prints, you will very likely find mine. Tennant was showing me his collection that afternoon.'

We all left the bungalow together and the inspector went off in his car. When I asked Bill where his car was he said, 'I walked here. Where are you going now?'

'Out to a farm several miles away,' I told him.

'I'll come with you,' he replied and minutes later I was heading away from the town.

'Am *I* suspect — having my dabs taken like that?' I asked.

'Not necessarily. It's a matter of eliminating the people they *don't* suspect.'

'I suppose that is meant to be comforting,' I answered ruefully.

Suddenly Bill grinned. 'Your inspector

is not really enamoured of having a private detective on the job, I believe. But he can't prevent me from coming in on the case.'

As I turned into a narrow country road Bill said, 'I am going to think aloud for a while. If you want to, chip in.'

'There are cigarettes in the front there by the dashboard,' I told him. 'No, I don't want one myself . . . '

He lit up and then said, 'That nurse is on my mind. Why did she really move the body when she *must* have known the old woman was dead? Why was she so insistent it was an accident when it is so obviously murder? And saying that abrasion was caused by falling on the door key . . . I have checked that Mrs Letts *didn't* fall towards it — not if, as they say her foot could be seen through the window.'

'You have reconstructed what could have happened?' I asked thoughtfully and then added, 'If she actually did think there was a spark of life . . . '

'Nurse Mackail is trained,' he broke in, 'she must have met death a good many times before — surely she must.'

'She is fairly young,' I answered. 'How about a policeman, for instance? *He* might be in the Force a good while before he met a murder. The same could apply to a nurse. Oh, dash it Bill — she strikes me as such a sincere sort of person.'

'A detective *never* goes on appearances,' Bill said quietly. He turned his head to glance at me. 'Have you a soft spot for this girl?' he asked.

'No — I haven't known her very long. But we ought to be fair to her. Especially when you quite obviously suspect her . . .'

He didn't reply at once. Then suddenly he said, 'You were saying when you first talked to me about this affair that there was little sign of any blood. That was because someone had cleared up after the murder. The floor had been pretty thoroughly washed and a carpet, obviously from the front part of the bungalow, put down. Now listen to this — the job was obviously done by candlelight — there were spots of grease on the floor. I remember you told me that Nurse

Mackail remarked there was no electricity in the kitchen.'

'Um . . . ' I said.

'And that they had to use *candles* out there,' Bill put in. 'Yet on her own admission she had never been in the house before that morning.'

'Um . . . ' I said again and Bill gave me a quick glance. 'Come on, tell me what you are thinking,' he ordered.

'She tried to persuade me there would be no need for an inquest . . . ' I related what had been said between us and added, 'The thing that worries me is that she might have got away with it too — if Dad had gone instead of myself, which is what she expected to happen because Mrs Letts was his patient. My Dad is not too well lately. It is possible *he* would not have made too thorough an examination.' I paused.

'Of course, many people *do* think a lot of unnecessary fuss is made when old folk trip — and die as a result. Especially if a doctor has been attending them, which, as Nurse Mackail pointed out to me, was so in this case. But, you see, Mrs Letts was *not* very old — only fifty-six.'

'She looked older than that?' Bill asked.

'Yes, for one thing she was quite grey-haired and she had put on a lot of weight — both things which give the appearance of age.'

'Very well then — this nurse could have assumed her patient to be old.' Now he *was* being fair to Nurse Mackail.

I stopped outside the farm where I had to visit a patient. When I got back to the car I found Bill just lighting up another cigarette. He was leaning back in his seat and did not speak or glance at me as I got into the driving seat and turned for our homeward journey. He appeared sunk in thought.

Perhaps he would have remained without 'thinking aloud' till we got back to Mewsdale, but at last I broke the silence myself. 'How about Tiny Bullen?' I demanded. 'He appears to have been the last one to see Mrs Letts alive.'

'Yes, but remember he volunteered that information himself.'

'Perhaps he felt it was safest to admit going there, just in case he was seen,' I replied. 'Still, I can't see that he had any motive.'

Bill drew on his cigarette for several seconds, then took it from between his lips and looked at it carefully before he remarked, 'It's not necessary to have a motive. Many murders are committed on the spur of the moment. In a fit of temper perhaps — with no premeditation and no motive whatsoever.'

'Has *anyone* connected with this case got a motive?' I asked.

'Not so far as I can see. Tennant owns what was obviously the murder weapon. There was human blood on the head of one of those sticks . . . '

I gave a small exclamation and Bill went on, 'Oh, someone imagined he or she had cleaned it all off, but it would be almost impossible to remove every trace from such an intricately carved piece of work. There was enough left to show it was of the same group as Mrs Letts'.'

'If the murderer used that as a weapon and cleaned it, then he must have taken off any fingerprints,' I suggested.

'No. Perhaps he — or she — thought

130

that might look suspicious. The blood was on the head of it. There are so many dabs on the stick itself that it will be a job to identify them all.'

'Mine are there I'm certain — as I told Inspector Gore.'

'And Tennant's without any doubt — but if you want a motive, I can't see he had one — quite the reverse. Mrs Letts had redecorated and refurnished part of her home to make him comfortable. He was happy there. Now, with only the daughter left, he may have to vacate his part of the bungalow.'

'You mean he has told you that Madeline may give him notice!' I exclaimed. 'That was not the impression I got from him.'

'He admitted to me that he feels he is in a very precarious position. Of course it has been impossible to question the daughter yet . . . '

'No, but I hope she will be better soon,' I told him.

We were back on the outskirts of Mewsdale. 'Want me to drop you off at The Lion?' I asked.

'No, take me round to the station,' he answered, glancing at his watch. 'I thought this little jaunt with you would nicely fill the time before the London train went. I'm off to find and talk to John Harvey — before the Inspector has a go at him. The train will be quicker than my car.'

'John Harvey,' I said thoughtfully. 'Of course I suppose he, too, is one of your suspects. No one saw him leave The Elms — not even Tiny Bullen . . . '

'No — and the police are bringing him back here for questioning. I want to get in just ahead of them,' he grinned.

As I drove towards the station approach I remarked, 'I can't imagine how you found out so much.'

'I have my methods,' Bill chuckled.

At the end of the morning I went along Rook Lane and saw that a couple of uniformed men were using a device that I recognised as a type of metal detector in the front garden of The Elms.

They were, possibly, looking for that front door key. But it was surely something they would never find . . .

8

My father and I had almost finished lunch when there was a ring at the bell and Miss Turner came to announce, 'Someone to see you — he won't give his name.'

I left the dining room and came face to face with — John Harvey. I admit I was startled. This was the man whom Bill had supposedly gone to London to see. 'How do *you* come to be here?' I asked.

'By train of course,' came the prompt reply.

That wasn't what I had meant. I led the way into my consulting room. 'It isn't surgery hours,' I remarked, 'but . . .'

'Oh, it isn't medical advice I want.' Harvey followed me and sat down in the chair I indicated.

'Has anyone interviewed you?' I asked him.

'No, no . . . I don't think the police would be very sympathetic. But I'm worried — and you were there that afternoon. Madeline Letts — I thought she was all right — but she's a snake-in-the-grass.'

Quite obviously he had not seen Bill or he would have said so.

He was sitting quite still on his chair, one hand resting on my desk — not clenched or tapping, as so often happened when a person was worked-up. His voice was forceful as he repeated, 'Yes, a snake-in-the-grass.'

'What do you mean?' I urged.

'Well, *she* says it was Tennant went with her in the car that afternoon. But it was *me*. Tennant was still there when we left. She said she'd run me to the station. He was hunting out some notes and told her he would come on in a few minutes — promised to meet her on the crossroads after she'd taken me to the train. I was afraid I was going to miss it.'

'Did you?'

'No — got it quite easily as it turned out.'

'Then probably someone saw you — the man in the ticket office . . . '

'I doubt it. That train is always crowded and people were pushing and shoving.'

'Do you often come down here?'

'No, of course not — only when Tennant wants me.' Harvey broke off and I said, 'Ralph Tennant has not been here long — he told me it was lucky you were coming so soon after he'd moved to The Elms. But you said that train is *always* crowded. How would you know?'

'I meant at that time of day trains are always packed. Now, don't *you* start picking on me . . . '

He looked at me and then down at his hand. 'I want you to tell me what to do,' he said. 'I'm worried. Is there any way I could put the screw on Madeline Letts to make her tell the truth?'

'You can't even see her at the moment,' I told him. 'She is ill.'

'Shamming, I suppose, because she doesn't want to see me . . . '

'No!' I interrupted. 'And her evidence at the inquest was very firm. She left with Tennant and at a time which coincided with Mr Bullen's statement — and *he* swore he saw them leave together.'

'It was getting dark. Inside the car he could just not be *sure* who he saw. And who does he say was driving?'

'It is only your word against three others,' I told him, and wondered why Harvey imagined he could convince me that *he*, instead of those others, was telling the truth. Why had he come to me — how did he think *I* could help him? But then, all sorts of folk *do* expect doctors and clergymen to work miracles . . .

I glanced at the man's swarthy face — the dark eyes set slightly too close together. He wasn't exactly a likeable type. In fact, suddenly, he reminded me of one of the jackals Tennant had shown us on his films . . .

I said abruptly, 'You knew Mrs Letts — before that day.'

'I knew her!' he exclaimed. 'I certainly did *not*.'

'Anyway, she knew you,' I insisted.

'Who told you that?' he demanded.

I didn't answer immediately and he brought his two hands together in an emphatic gesture. 'I didn't know that

136

woman from Adam,' he declared.

'But you knew someone of the same name — you said so — and wished afterwards you had not been so impulsive. *I* believe it was really Mrs Letts you meant, even though you did not admit it. Perhaps you wanted to stay behind that evening. Perhaps it was for you she was making the casserole . . . '

He stood up. He swore angrily. 'Who do you think you are — a ruddy detective?' he demanded.

'No. Calm down, and sit down again,' I said. 'I tried that out on you because that is the sort of thing the police will probably say to you — and what do you imagine they will think if you react like that?' He was still standing up. 'You came to me for advice — well, I will give it to you. Go to the police. Tell them exactly what you have told me — if it's the truth . . . '

He broke angrily into my sentence. 'Of course it's the truth,' he insisted.

I was silent and after a moment or two he calmed down. 'Well, look here, if I go,' he began, but all at once the phone bell cut into what he was saying.

Seconds later I was telling him, 'Sorry — I'll have to go now. But you take my advice and go to see the police.'

'All — right. I — will,' he promised.

I picked up my case and Harvey went ahead of me out into the hall. I put my head in at the dining room door to tell Dad, 'I shall not be able to finish my lunch — have to go out in a hurry. But I'll be back to pick you up as soon as I can.'

When I got back to the front door Harvey had opened it and I followed him into the porch. Then I saw Nurse Mackail hurrying along the garden path towards us. 'Oh, Doctor,' she said, even before she reached me. 'I've just caught you. I want to see you about that Jones case you sent me to . . . '

'That's not urgent,' I told her.

'No . . . o . . . o.'

'But the case I have just been called to is,' I stated. I had not stopped. As I met and passed her I added, 'I'm sorry — you'll have to come back and see me later.'

I went to the garage, started up my car

and began to back out. As I edged my way across the pavement I saw that Harvey and the nurse were talking together. She was holding her cycle, one foot on a pedal, as though she was in a hurry to be off.

At lunch time I had persuaded Dad to let me take him with me on my afternoon round. So, after attending to the emergency, I returned home. I found my father in the sitting room gazing out at the garden. His hands were clasped limply behind his back. 'Ready?' I asked. 'Remember — I was going to take you along for a chat with old Underhill . . . ' I planned to drop him at Tom's place, and pick him up again on my way home.

'Oh — yes,' Dad agreed now. He did not sound very enthusiastic, but I knew that once he started talking to the old man he would forget himself for a while.

As I got into the car I decided to go round via the police station and tell them of Harvey's visit to me. Bill had said *they*, like himself, intended going to London in order to see the man. I must let them know that Harvey was in their own vicinity.

It was fairly late when I got back to Tom Underhill's place. The old man greeted me with his usual toothless but attractive smile. He said, 'I was just talking to Dr. Jax about this murder — dreadful thing to happen. I used to live next door to the Letts — when they first came here that was — oh, can't reckon how many years ago now . . . '

I had not long to spare but I could not just walk out on the old boy the minute I arrived, so for a short while I let him ramble on with his reminiscences but as soon as I could I escaped, taking Dad with me. Tom had talked to him about the murder — something I had not done — but Dad did not mention it on the way home.

I had almost finished my tea when Nurse Mackail came back but since I had been in the practice I had got used to interruptions at any hour of the day or night. Philosophically I left a meal for the second time that day. At anyrate, whatever it was the nurse wanted to discuss would not take long. It didn't and I stood up — eager to get back before my cup of tea was cold.

Nurse Mackail stood up too, but she did not move towards the door. She asked abruptly, 'What did that man Harvey want with you?'

'You must know, Nurse, that a doctor does not discuss his patients.'

'*He* is not your patient. He doesn't live in Mewsdale.'

'It is not only residents who need a doctor,' I retorted, trying to keep my patience.

'*He* is not ill,' she said. She was not looking at me.

'He came about the murder, didn't he? Tell me what he wanted with you.'

'Nurse Mackail I think you are forgetting yourself!' I exclaimed. She glanced at me then — and went quickly towards the door. Perhaps my face had shown my wrath — I know I *felt* angry.

We neither of us spoke as we went along the hall. I opened the door to let her out. She raised her eyes as she passed me. 'Goodbye, Nurse,' I said, but she did not reply.

I don't think she liked me much — that woman. The feeling was reciprocated.

After a particularly busy surgery I settled down with a medical journal and hoped I would have no more interruptions that day. But before long the doorbell rang. I went to answer it myself. Bill Rice was outside. 'Come on in,' I invited, and led the way back into my study. As I closed the door I said, 'Pity you had a wild goose chase to London today.'

'Oh, it wasn't that,' he told me. 'I did find out some useful information there. Sorry — can't tell you what at the moment.'

'I thought I ought to let them know at the station about Harvey coming here,' I said. 'I advised him to go to them. I wonder if he has?'

'Not so far. I have been to find out if they'd seen him.'

'Then suppose he's hooked it?'

'He won't get far,' Bill smiled.

'You think now that *he* was the one who killed Mrs Letts,' I suggested.

Bill's smile still lingered. '*Did* I give you that idea? Sorry — at the moment I can't say who did it. But everyone connected with her has to be questioned.'

I told him how Nurse Mackail had come at lunch time and about her subsequent visit. Then I said, 'I was over at Tom Underhill's this afternoon and he related a bit of ancient history about Mrs Letts. I don't suppose it would be of any interest to you . . . '

'You may as well let me have it,' Bill said.

'Well, when the Letts first came to Mewsdale they went to live next door to Tom — that must be about thirty years ago because they had moved over to the bungalow before Madeline was born and she is about my age. Now, when they came they had a small boy with them. At first Tom thought the child was theirs but after a few weeks he disappeared. Tom had got used by then to the small face peeping through the fence at him, watching him in his garden, and he asked Mrs Letts if her boy was ill. 'He's not mine,' she said. 'He's my sister's child.

She's going out to Australia and we've only had him while they've been settling up. So you won't ever see him again.' And Tom never did. But as soon as he heard about the Letts' case now he remembered that 'boy with the thin face,' as he put it.'

Bill was looking thoughtful. 'Daresay it *is* irrelevant history,' he said, 'but thanks for handing it on.'

'Going back to John Harvey,' I remarked. 'I must tell you what he said to me.' I related what had passed between us and finished, 'Somehow I doubt that he *did* go on that train, as he says. He was emphatic that it was unlikely anyone saw him in the crush and he used a word which struck me very much — he said *always* the train was crowded at that time. It slipped out I think. He didn't want to admit that he had been in Mewsdale before, yet I feel sure he had.'

'I'll have a go at finding out,' Bill answered thoughtfully. 'He must have gone back to London by *some* means that evening, too, seeing he didn't have a car. Another thing has just struck me. Tonsford is on the way to London. You might have thought he would have gone that far with Tennant and the girl . . . '

It was fairly late when at last Bill stood up to go. Our talk had strayed far from any crime or medical subject — something that was probably good for me. In the course of our reminiscing I had been able to forget the shadow which seemed to hang over Roseville. But not for long could I forget. As I went into the hall with Bill my father came in at the front door. I had imagined him to be in the sitting room when my friend arrived, thought he would have been in bed long before now.

I said, 'Hullo Dad.' But it was almost as though he did not see me. Bill held out his hand. 'Nice to see you, Dr Jax,' he remarked. He might have been addressing a blind man. Dad took no heed of the outstretched hand but went on to the foot of the stairs where he halted and stood looking up — almost as though he could see someone coming down towards him. Several times I had watched him do this before, and I wondered if it was my mother *he* could see.

From the doorway Bill looked back. 'I

think I understand what you meant when you said your father was not at all well lately. The loss of your mother must have been a great shock to him,' he said slowly.

'Yes, but . . . '

No, I couldn't put into words what I felt. Dad had always been a strong character. I had loved him and I had respected him. He had despised weakness so, somehow, it seemed incredible that even a great sorrow could break him . . . I should have expected him to stick his chin out and up. Instead it was often, in a manner of speaking, down on his chest.

I felt a surge of bitter disappointment. Only this afternoon I had been telling myself that at last he was getting back to being his old self. And *where* had he been tonight? It would be useless to ask . . .

9

I was turning into the gateway of a house in the main street next morning when I saw Tiny Bullen hurrying towards me. There was anger in each of his quick jerky strides and his long, gaunt face was red. I tried to escape into my patient's house but Tiny called to me and I could not ignore his urgent shout. I asked sharply. 'Is anything the matter? What is the trouble?'

'Trouble enough,' he said. 'You know my beautiful holly arch — over my gateway. Someone's broken it down — pulled great pieces out of it — ruined it . . . '

'Hooligans,' I sympathized.

'Young wretches. You wouldn't think *anyone* would mess about with a prickly holly hedge. The work I've put into cutting and training . . . Years of work . . . ' He was still raging as he left me and I realised he was making for the police station.

Later that day I saw John Harvey. He was pedalling towards me on a bicycle, but turned off before he reached me into a road that led towards a lonely farmhouse.

For a moment I felt tempted to follow him . . . overtake him . . . But if I did, what should I say? Ask him if he *had* gone to the police? Once already he had accused me of trying to be a 'ruddy detective.' It was the Inspector's job to sort out this affair. He — and Bill — probably knew, anyway, that Harvey was still in the district. It was my job to be a doctor. I must think about my patients and forget John Harvey.

But that was not so easy. When I was returning home a couple of hours later I saw him again — this time with Nurse Mackail. They did not see me. Their cycles were propped against a hedge and the two of them were, side by side, leaning on a gate to look across a ploughed field where sea gulls fluttered and swooped in a ragged cloud of black and white. Most probably the noisy screeching of the birds would have

148

blotted out the sound of my engine . . .

But Nurse Mackail on friendly terms with 'that Mr Harvey' as she had called him? Was *this* something I ought to tell Bill?

*   *   *

That evening Tennant came to my surgery. He was the last, Mrs Watson told me as she showed him in. I remembered that the first time I saw him he had been my final patient . . .

I asked, 'What can I do for you?'

He sat down in the chair on the further side of my desk and, resting his chin in his hands, looked across at me. 'I hope you don't mind me coming to the surgery,' he said, 'but I feel I want to talk to someone.'

I remembered again that time when I had first made his acquaintance, and how glad I had been to talk to *him*. 'Of course I don't mind,' I said.

'You think Madeline will be all right, don't you?' he asked.

'She will be quite all right — given

care,' I answered.

'Well — I don't know — she had dreadful nightmares last night — scared Mrs Hodgson with her moans and shouts . . . '

I couldn't imagine that saturnine woman being scared. I asked, 'Why didn't *she* tell me about this? I was round at The Elms this morning.'

Ralph Tennant moved his elbow from the desk and, slipping a packet of cigarettes form his pocket flipped it open and offered me one. We both lit up before he went on quietly, 'Truth to tell, I'm worried about Madeline. I mean, losing her mother the way she did. It wouldn't affect her brain, would it?'

Memory flashed a quick picture through my mind of the way Madeline had treated her mother on the afternoon of my visit. I recalled how uneasy the girl had been this morning. Could remorse — or something deeper unhinge her mind? I pushed the thought away.

'Good heavens, no!' I exclaimed. 'I have known her longer than you have, Tennant. Madeline is too level-headed to go out of her mind — even after a big shock.'

'That's a relief, then,' he said after a pause. 'I'm very fond of her, you understand.'

I didn't reply and he asked at last, 'Have they got any further with their enquiries into the murder?'

'I haven't heard anything,' I told him.

'Doesn't the affair puzzle you?' he demanded. 'I mean, Mrs Letts was such a harmless old soul. Who would want to hurt her?'

'I have kept asking myself that question,' I answered. 'You wouldn't know if she was fairly well-off — despite her apparent poverty?'

'How *could* I know that?'

'You are very friendly with Madeline,' I suggested. 'She might have told you. And, being ill, she can't be questioned herself. The thing that occured to me was that robbery might have been the motive . . . '

'Ah . . . yes . . . ' Tennant sounded thoughtful. 'That could be the case, I suppose. The only fact I know is that she had a pension — the same as I know Mr Bullen has one. *He* had the idea it would be fine if he and Mrs Letts joined forces. Madeline heard him telling her mother so one day, persuading her that when two people live together it doubled their income but halved their out-goings.

'I imagine there is something a trifle wrong with that theory,' I smiled. 'And apparently Mrs Letts did not agree to his proposal.'

'Not so far she hadn't — but old Bullen is the sort who does not give up easily. I know. I didn't want him pushing in and 'helping' when I moved in, but neither persuasion nor downright rudeness could make him desist.'

Usually I enjoyed talking to Ralph Tennant but tonight I was tired, and I certainly did not want to chatter about Tiny Bullen. In the end I stood up and said that my supper would be getting cold and that I had to go out in less than half an hour.

★ ★ ★

I did not see Bill again for a couple of days. Then we were both in the bank at the same time and, leaving together, we walked along towards the place where we had been forced to park our cars. It was market day — when residents had difficulty in getting a vehicle anywhere near the centre of the town.

We were silent as we pushed our way along the crowded pavements. Then suddenly Bill stopped, his gaze riveted on someone ahead of us ... someone who was wearing a fawn coat and had fair hair which tossed up and down as she hurried along. Gwenda! Gwenda, out at this time of the morning ... I shrugged my surprise away. She had never told me that her employer sent her out on an errand, but that was obviously what had happened now.

I had stopped beside Bill but I began to walk on again and he moved too. But his eyes were still watching Gwenda, who was making much more headway than we were, her slim figure darting agilely between the jostling crowds.

Bill said, 'I hope you will forgive me,

Ian, but I intend to follow your sister. Do you want to come too?'

'For heaven's sake, why?' I exploded.

'I don't know but I've got a feeling that I should. It's a sort of extra sense we detectives develop. Please try not to be angry, Ian.'

I calmed down. After all, I had asked Bill to come in on this case. I should be willing to trust him. 'All right,' I agreed. 'I'll come with you.'

Quickening our steps a little we followed Gwenda the whole length of the street and then across the bridge. She turned into the road which led down to the river. There were no crowds here — only a solitary car at the end of it — a Singer, which was facing away from us.

Bill beckoned me to stay behind one of the huge piers of the bridge, from where we could watch without being seen. I felt despicable, following Gwenda like this, but if Bill had some good reason for it who was I to question him?

Gwenda reached the car, leaned towards it and thrust her hand through the open window. She appeared to be handing in something white but, from our distance, I could not tell what it was. She withdrew her hand, turned and walked quickly back in our direction.

I did not want her to know we had followed her. I turned, intending to move away before she reached us. But Bill put out a restraining hand. And so we remained, hidden by the bridge, and watched Gwenda go by — so close to us that we could have touched her.

She did not see us. Still hurrying, her cheeks pink from exertion, her eyes gazed straight ahead of her. She seemed oblivious of everything but, perhaps, her own thoughts.

We waited quite quietly for several seconds before Bill turned, but not to follow Gwenda this time. He said, 'I think I would like to talk to the person in that car.'

With a last glance in my sister's direction, I began to walk again at his side. I was startled by his sudden exclamation. 'Damn!' he said, 'we are too late.'

The car was starting to move away from us . . . gathering speed . . . It turned left at the first intersection and we could no longer see it.

'No good trying to follow it,' he said. 'Know whose car it was — did you recognise it at all?'

'Tennant has a Singer like it,' I volunteered, 'but I couldn't be sure it was his.'

'Could you find out if it was? Mention to Gwenda casually that you saw her this morning. She might make some explanation.'

'I wish all this business could be settled up,' I told him. 'Have you *any* idea who the murderer was?'

'At the moment, I may as well admit to you, I have no clear suspect,' he answered. 'Oh, there is another way I'd like you to help me. You say Madeline Letts is better, but I've had no chance to speak to her. I think, though, you would be able to chat to her casually and find out something — about what you told me yourself, as a matter of fact. Try to discover if her mother has any relatives in

Australia or anywhere abroad, for that matter.'

We had reached the place where I had parked my car and, before Bill went on to his own, he halted to say, 'John Harvey is staying in Mewsdale — at a small boarding house. I had a bother to corner him but I managed it yesterday. He wouldn't say much, though.'

'I've seen him talking to Nurse Mackail a couple of times,' I said, 'but I don't suppose there would be any significance in that, though she seemed not to like him.'

Bill shrugged. 'They are about a lot together,' he replied, and then returned to the subject of Madeline.

'I'll let you know if you *can* talk to her after I've seen her today,' I promised.

I had a feeling of aversion about questioning either of the girls, as Bill Rice had suggested to me. Yet, as it happened, I obtained the information he wanted from Madeline almost without asking for it. When I went to see her that afternoon she was obviously a lot better. Mrs Hodgson was in the kitchen and had gestured me to go on in. The bedroom door was ajar and Madeline had seen me arriving. She called, 'Come in, Ian.'

As I crossed the floor towards her I was very conscious of the unease indicated by her restless hands, of the expression in her eyes which betrayed disquiet. 'You are specially worried about something,' I stated without preamble.

'No.' But the denial was not very firm and I pressed, 'You are working yourself up about Inspector Gore coming here.'

'No . . . Oh, I *wish* I had someone to advise me — I mean some sort of relative. I seem so — all alone. And I don't like Mrs Hodgson. She gives me the creeps.'

'You don't *have* to keep her.'

'But I can't stay on my own — and who else could I get?'

That was a question I couldn't answer, so I was silent for a moment or two before I remarked, 'Haven't you got an aunt or *anyone?*'

'No, my mother was an only child — I've heard her say she wished she had a sister or a brother.'

'So you haven't any relations in England?'

'No.'

'Or any even abroad anywhere — Australia . . . '

'Of course not — if I haven't got uncles or aunts or cousins, what relations *could* I have — anywhere in the world?'

So it would appear that Tom's story of a sister emigrating to Australia was not right — unless, for some reason, Mrs Letts had deliberately not told her daughter about it. I said, 'If you want any advice that I could give you . . . '

'I don't know.' She looked up at me. The expression in her eyes at that moment was unreadable. She said, 'Ian, you are not only a friend but my doctor as well. On both those counts can I talk to you in confidence — knowing you won't discuss what I say to anyone? You see, it seems impossible to make up my mind. Perhaps that is just because I am not well.'

'Then leave making any decision till you are better — that is my advice.'

'It's not as easy as that,' she said. She

159

was speaking in a whisper. I guessed she wanted to make sure Mrs Hodgson did not hear what she told me. 'It's like this — I haven't got any money — no ready cash at all . . . '

As she paused I asked, 'Was there no insurance?'

'Not more than enough for the funeral expenses. I was a bit shocked over that. I thought Mum paid insurance and imagined I would get a bit.' Again she paused before she added, 'There is nothing. Mum was always a bit secretive about her affairs but once she told me her grandfather had left her a legacy . . . '

'That could have meant anything,' I said, 'even just a picture or a bit of china.'

'Surely she would have shown me that. No, I'm convinced she meant money — she said it was a legacy I would get one day.'

'Then the bungalow,' I suggested.

'Oh no. That is mine — I've known that a long time, but my father bought it, tying it up in some sort of legal way that it was Mum's as long as she lived — but came to me on her death. No, the bungalow was nothing to do with the legacy my mother talked about.'

I said, 'Even a few hundreds can easily disappear in these days of high costs. It might have gone a pound at a time — or . . . ' I hesitated. 'It must have cost Mrs Letts a certain amount to have the place redecorated a little while ago.'

'Yes — of course . . . ' She glanced swiftly round the room. Faded wallpaper, chipped paintwork, old dressing table and wardrobe which did not match . . . one threadbare rug on worn lino . . . 'This is not a room to be proud of, is it?' she asked.

But she did not wait for me to answer. She hurried on, 'You know what my mother's room is like — I'll have to do something about that. Now, could I take up a mortgage on the bungalow? Would I be allowed to do that and spend the money on renovations? Would it be a good idea, Ian?'

'Well yes,' I had to agree, 'folk do often raise money that way to improve their property. Providing you know you have the means of being able to make the repayments . . . '

'I haven't even got a job at the moment,' she said.

'Then leave it till you have,' I advised her. After all, the place had been in a pickle for some while. It could stay that way a bit longer. I said, 'Listen, Madeline, I think you ought to try getting up. You are better now . . . '

'You mentioned Inspector Gore just now,' she said. 'I suppose he *does* still want to see me?'

'Yes, and the sooner you get it over the better,' I told her. 'There is absolutely nothing at all for you to worry about.'

'Ian, you said that with such conviction. Has the inspector *told* you . . . I mean, does he think he knows who . . . who . . . ' Her voice trailed away She couldn't put into words the terrible thing that had happened to her mother.

I said firmly, 'You asked for my advice. This is it — don't worry about the bungalow or anything else till you are better, and see Inspector Gore as soon as possible. When you have faced that you will get better more quickly. Shall I tell him to come along tomorrow?'

When she began to protest I said, 'Listen — tell the truth and you will be all right. And here's a promise — I'll come along to see you myself when they have gone to make sure you are all right and give you a sedative, if necessary. I don't think it will be.'

When I went to The Elms next afternoon I took Bill with me, but made him wait outside till I had gone in to find out how Madeline was. Her cheeks were flushed but she seemed quite cheerful. 'I shan't want your old sedative,' she told me.

'Good. Now, do you feel equal to seeing a friend of mine? He's a detective, but a private one . . . '

For a moment I thought she would refuse. Then she agreed, 'All right.' And I fetched Bill in.

She was sitting in a chair by her bed, her back to the window, a blanket wrapped round her. I said, 'This is Mr Rice. What he wants to ask you won't take long.'

I had already relayed to him the

information I had managed to get about her mother's relatives. Now Bill said, 'First of all I'd like you to try and recall what happened when Dr Jax left here on Thursday the . . . '

'I know the date,' she broke in. 'Do you think I can ever forget it?'

I said placatingly, 'I left here about five o' clock.'

'Yes — and John Harvey went about three quarters of an hour later. He said he was going to walk to the station. I offered to drive him but he refused — insisted he'd like the exercise.'

Tiny Bullen averred he had not seen Harvey either go in or leave. Of course, just at the moment he might not have been watching . . .

'And not long after that you left?' Bill suggested. 'You were going to Tonsford . . . '

'Yes, where Ralph had to give a lecture,' Madeline agreed.

'What time did you leave the house?'

'I couldn't say to the minute — but I remember I put my watch on when I was ready to leave and I set it right with

Ralph's clock at five to six. We would have been away — oh, only a minute or two afterwards.'

'We?' Bill prodded.

Madeline was not looking at him but watching her own first finger as she drew it back and forth across the blanket on her knees. She asked, 'What are you trying to make me say?'

'Nothing but the truth,' Bill answered quietly. 'You left here at just on six o'clock with . . . '

'Ralph, of course,' she said.

'Which of you put the light out in the sitting room?'

She appeared startled by that question. 'I suppose — well, I suppose Ralph did. He . . . he always came out behind me, but I'm not *sure* he put it out. I remember asking him if he had switched it off — when we were about half-way to Tonsford.'

'Did he often forget to put it out?'

'No. But you know how it is — you do things automatically — and then afterwards you wonder if it has been done . . . '

165

'Yes,' Bill agreed, and then after a pause, 'Do you remember your father?'

'Why ever do you ask that?'

'I'd just like to know.'

I thought Madeline was going to refuse to answer but after a moment she said, 'I was only four when he died — is it likely I should remember him?'

'Do you know what he was like?'

'Not very good — if what my mother said was true. He used to go away to work a lot. When he did that he didn't allow her any money or precious little.'

'Do you know what he looked like?'

'No — I remember once asking Mum if she had a photo of him and she said *if* she had it would have been burnt long ago. She wanted to forget him and would I allow her to do it . . . ' Madeline broke off. I believe she had almost forgotten she was talking to Bill. She looked very young, huddled in her chair, with her hair around her shoulders. I felt sorry for her.

She went on slowly, 'I must have been about ten or eleven then. It was the only time I ever really heard her talk about him. I don't know why she did that day — except that I had been curious and asked questions. But in the end she seemed angry that she *had* been induced to talk. She told me never to mention him again — and I never did.' Her restless finger had slowed. Now it stilled completely as she added, 'She said that day she'd never have another man inside her door.'

'But she did,' Bill remarked. 'Mr Bullen came here.'

'*Pushed* in here.' The ghost of a smile touched Madeline's lips. 'Do you know Busybody Bullen? Have you ever tried to keep him out when he meant to come in?'

Bill grinned. 'I don't know him very well, but I can guess what he is like.' He paused. He was looking beyond Madeline to the window but suddenly his glance came back to her as he asked abruptly, 'Your mother allowed Mr Tennant to come and *live* in her home — how did he persuade her to let that happen?'

'I don't know really. I met him in a pub first. I guess I must have been extra drunk at our next meeting, for I told him about the sort of shambles I lived in — something I usually kept very quiet. I never brought anyone here — but he made me bring him.' She paused. 'I think he was shocked when I told him. I know he was sorry for me.'

She looked up. 'I've been grateful to Ralph ever since.'

'Haven't you any idea how he achieved the miracle?'

'He told me once he had threatened to report her to the R.S.P.C.A. for cruelty to animals — me being the animal and having to live in such a pigsty. I knew that was his joke, of course, but I asked her if that was what he'd done and she said 'something like that'. But she wouldn't say any more. Anyway, she paid up to have all the work done. Mind you he will never admit it but I'm sure he gave Mum the money afterwards. He's like that — doing good by stealth.'

'Money?' Bill asked. 'Do you know if any was stolen — that night?'

Madeline shook her head. 'I don't know what she had — so if any was taken I wouldn't be any the wiser.' She put both her hands palm down on the bed.

'Madeline is getting terribly tired,' I said. 'She must rest now.'

Immediately Bill stood up. 'All right — we will go,' he said, 'and thank you for being so co-operative.'

Out in the passage the connecting door between back and front of the bungalow was closed and Mrs Hodgson stood in front of it — almost as though she was on guard, I thought. Bill asked, 'Mr Tennant in?'

'No.'

I said, 'Will you go to Miss Letts, please? Make her get back into bed and rest now — but she can get up tomorrow earlier.'

Mrs Hodgson was gesturing Bill to go out the way we had come in — through the kitchen and back doorway. I followed him. As we reached Bill's car I said, 'Ever heard a taller tale than that — about reporting Mrs Letts . . . '

'Ah, not to the society mentioned perhaps,' he put in. 'But there are Health Inspectors, you know — to the people of her mentality the threat of a visit from the sanitary inspector is even worse than that of one from the police.'

We had both been standing with our back to the bungalow. Suddenly Bill spun round and then began to walk quickly back along the drive to the front door.

10

Bill's movements had startled me. He had made no explanation for his hasty return towards the bungalow. For a moment I hesitated. Then I followed him. He rang the bell on the front door and called, 'Tennant, you wanted me? You were beckoning to me from the window . . . '

There was no reply. 'Tennant, what's wrong?' Bill rattled the handle. 'Are you all right? Ian, you go round to the back. When someone beckons to you and then disappears . . . '

But I had no time to move before the door opened and Tennant stood inside. 'What's all the fuss about?' he demanded.

'You tried to attract my attention,' Bill said.

'I did nothing of the sort,' Ralph retorted.

'At any rate I'd like to come in.'

The man inside was obviously unwilling to open the door any wider, but Bill

171

moved a step nearer. A moment or two later we were in Tennant's sitting room. Bill glanced round and then walked deliberately across to peer behind the large settee.

'What's that in aid of?' Tennant asked.

'I haven't forgotten that one murder was committed in this place,' Bill told him grimly. 'I just wondered if you were being threatened by someone — and that was the reason you were being so reluctant to let us in.'

'That someone might have been in here covering me with a gun?' Ralph asked.

Bill had returned to the door. 'Mind if I look in the bedroom?' he asked, in a low voice. Tennant shook his head and Bill moved quietly across the passage, flung open the bedroom door. He waited for a moment, then dropped on all fours and crawled quickly forward. I know I was tensed for the sound of a shot, but it did not come. Moments afterwards Bill was back in the sitting room.

Tennant said, 'If you'd only put your hands on the murderer then we'd all feel safer. I should imagine the man was miles away from here by now, but I can't get Madeline to take that view. All the time she lives on tenterhooks.'

'Madeline, yes,' Bill said. 'When you left here that Thursday evening, was she driving the car?'

Did Ralph hesitate — uncertain what to reply? And why hadn't Bill asked *her* that question? Because he'd had to leave before he had the chance?

Tennant said at last, 'I was driving of course.'

'But she could drive?'

'Oh yes.'

'And has driven several times when you left here?'

There was another pause. Then, 'Yes,' came the almost reluctant admission, followed by, 'I can't think what that could have to do with solving a murder.'

'It's just that one statement has to be checked against another,' Bill told him.

'Oh? Then does someone say Madeline was driving that evening? Old Bullen . . .' He broke off. 'No, Bullen says he saw us go, so it must be someone else. Who?'

Bill said, 'May we sit down?'

'I suppose so.'

I had the feeling we were not at all welcome today.

Bill asked suddenly, 'How did you manage to persuade Mrs Letts to have all this work done here?' When Tennant did not reply at once my friend remarked, 'You must know what a seven-day wonder it caused all round here. Everyone declared the bungalow had been a disgrace to the neighbourhood for years. Then you came along and . . . '

'It was easy,' Ralph said into the sudden silence. 'Mrs Letts was a charming old soul.'

Charming? That was not the impression she gave me the afternoon I came here. I could see her now coming through the doorway, carrying that loaded tray . . .

Perhaps Tennant could read my thoughts — or *he* remembered that I must have seen how morose and unattractive she appeared that day. He said, 'Underneath an intimidating exterior there is often a lamb instead of a wolf — if you only know the right approach.'

'And what *is* that?' Bill asked. 'After all,

Mrs Letts was Madeline's mother, and if a daughter could not get under the crust, it's difficult to see how a stranger could.'

Tennant laughed then. 'You forget I'm no ordinary stranger,' he returned. 'I have lived in the jungle. A lion could seem a frightening proposition to most folk but I have had a tame one around my camp.'

'So you'd apply the same technique to subduing a human as you would to taming a lion or wolf?'

'A human is only another sort of animal.'

'But one who has ears to listen to a threat — and a brain to appreciate the significance and far-reaching consequences of it if carried out,' Bill suggested.

'What *do* you mean?'

'Madeline says you threatened her mother . . . '

The man's forehead creased in a frown before he gave another laugh. 'Oh, I remember! She didn't repeat that stupid joke of mine!'

Bill began, 'I suggest . . . '

But Tennant broke in, 'Now listen, I

used no threats — it's a ridiculous thing to insinuate. What the old girl did, she did willingly.'

'But only for you — not for herself . . . '

He shrugged. 'I suppose she *liked* all her wretched junk.' He glanced towards the sideboard. 'A drink?' he offered.

'No, no thank you,' Bill said. 'Have one yourself, though.'

'That *would* be unsociable. A cup of tea or coffee, perhaps? I'll give Mrs Hodgson a shout.'

'No, don't bother.' Bill stood up. 'Mrs Hodgson,' he said. 'She knew you were in today?'

Again that pause, as though he was considering whether to say yes or no . . . Then Ralph answered, 'Yes, yes, she knew.'

'Then why did she tell us you were out?'

'I don't know.'

'You instructed her to say so.'

'No!' Tennant looked angry now.

Bill turned to the door and, reaching it, switched the light on and off. He asked,

'Can you recall which of you switched this off when you left the bungalow on the night of the murder?'

'No.'

'Who usually did it?'

'I don't know — either of us, I suppose — whichever left the room last.'

'Were you usually last?'

'I don't know.'

'Suppose you got well away from the bungalow — would you worry about it if you had left it on?'

'I don't imagine so.'

'Would Madeline fuss about it?'

'Madeline? I don't know. These damn questions! Haven't you asked enough?'

'Just one more — did Madeline ask you on the way to Tonsford that evening if you had left it on?'

'On the way . . . I don't know. I can't remember.'

* * *

When we had left the bungalow and the door had closed behind us with a small thud, I said to Bill, 'You don't think

Madeline *did* ask about the light, do you? But why would she have made up a thing like that?'

'I could make a good guess,' he said, 'but guesses are no good. I have to know.'

We reached the roadway. Further along I saw Nurse Mackail pushing her cycle across the pavement and into a gateway. For a moment she paused, glancing in our direction. I thought she was going to move towards us. Bill had seen her too. He said, 'Nurse Mackail is always such a busy person — always needed by her patients but for once I have caught her coming home.'

He moved hurriedly away from me. 'Perhaps at last I can take up a small slice of the leisure she has always before denied having . . . '

As I got into my car I saw him disappear through the gateway of the house where the nurse lived.

I had meant to tell him how I had tried to question Gwenda diplomatically about her meeting with someone in that car — yet what was there to report? I couldn't admit I had spied on her. I simply said I thought I had seen her in town that morning — and she had flatly denied being there. I was puzzled and distressed. In the old days my sister would not have stooped to even a 'white lie'.

11

I recognised Ralph Tennant's voice on the other end of the wire. 'It's Madeline,' he said. 'I wonder if you would call in some time today? Nothing very urgent, but I'm a bit worried about her. Don't make a special journey — oh, and don't tell her I phoned you.'

'She has seemed such a lot better. Since she began getting up, she has appeared to improve so well. We can't have her ill again — but don't worry. I shall be along your road later in the day. I'll look in then,' I promised.

'Good, will it be during the morning or afternoon?' he asked. 'Mrs Hodgson wants some time off, and I'd like to be here when you call. I'd like a chat with you about Madeline. She seeems so very depressed. Perhaps you could think of some way I could help her.'

I told him I would be at the bungalow about five that afternoon, on my way back from a hospital visit, but it was actually only a quarter to the hour when I reached The Elms. As I stepped out of my car and went along the drive to the front door I was thinking that perhaps the most obvious way Tennant could help Madeline was by marrying her very soon.

They seemed quite a well-matched couple. She took a great interest in his lectures, and I could imagine she would be more than willing to accompany him on his trips abroad. In fact, for him to take her off for the unusual adventure of a safari in Africa would be a wonderful way to make her forget the horror of what had happened to her mother.

I had just reached the front door and was about to put my finger on the bell when I heard footsteps and Ralph Tennant came round the side of the building. 'Hullo, Doctor,' he said. 'I did not expect you just yet. I thought you said five o'clock.'

'My visit did not take as long as I imagined it would,' I explained.

He made no attempt to open the door for me but, instead, turned and started to walk towards the rear of the bungalow. I followed him, but he did not turn in the direction of the back door — he went on along the garden path. I hesitated, wondering if I should continue to follow him or go on in to see Madeline. He had asked me to come and visit her . . .

Then he looked back at me, slowing for me to overtake him. When I reached him he said, 'I thought we could talk better away from the house.'

Of course — he had said he wanted to talk about Madeline, and inside the bungalow he was afraid she might have heard . . .

I glanced round me. How well I remembered this garden from the times when we had played truant from home and come here with Madeline, thinking this much more attractive than our own well-ordered plot. Here the weeds ran riot among gorse bushes, and the trees were wonderful for climbing. Beyond the garden, separated only by a barbed wire fence, was The Wood. We always gave it capitals because it was such a magical place for games — and beyond it was The

Pond — deep enough for sailing our boats. Too deep for us to play around, my mother had said, when she discovered we had been there one day.

Nostalgically the memories returned. Ralph Tennant's voice cut into my reverie. 'It was only indirectly I wanted to talk to you about Madeline,' he said. 'You see, I think if we can get all these enquiries cleared up she will eventually forget all about her mother's tragic death. She never will with police around all the time.'

'You care for her a lot, don't you?' I suggested.

'I care enough to wish this damned business was finished with,' he admitted. We were about halfway down the path and he stopped suddenly, breaking a small branch off the high thick hedge which enclosed the garden on both sides. I watched him pull the leaves from the twig and throw them to the ground as he went on talking.

He said, 'I have a theory and some evidence to uphold it. I wanted to ask you first if you think it is important enough to tell the inspector. I do want the case cleared up but I don't enjoy having him poking around and upsetting Madeline. So if you think my theory is way out, tell me and I'll drop it.'

'*Any* evidence is important to the police,' I told him. 'This case is nothing to do with me.' And yet, as I spoke the words, I knew they were an untruth. Gwenda was involved in this murder somehow. And if Gwenda was mixed up in it then it was, desperately, to do with me. If Ralph Tennant had some proof that would bring the murderer to justice, surely I should not refuse to hear about it . . .

I said, 'The police have been pretty thorough, but it is possible for them to overlook vital clues, I suppose.'

'Well, they took it for granted the murderer left the bungalow through the front gate, but I don't think he would have done that. Why should he, when there was this way out with no danger of anyone seeing him?' His voice was level and quiet, carrying conviction. I wondered why Gore had not thought of this obvious fact.

Ralph went on, 'I came down here earlier today because I was thinking about tidying up a bit. This place is almost like a jungle — the weeds are so high.'

He halted, gazing around and then looking at me, waving his hand towards a pathway of trampled bramble and grass. 'I pushed my way through there to the fence at the bottom — it is very rusty barbed wire, and, caught on one of the barbs, I discovered a tiny strand of tweed.'

'Did you recognise it at all — remember any coat it might have come from?' I asked.

'That's not up to me to say, but I left it there. I wanted you to see it before I told anyone else about it.'

I was suddenly eager to see this strand of material, and knew that my eagerness was tied up with the knowledge that *Gwenda* did not possess a tweed coat . . .

I stepped past Ralph and went on towards the bottom of the garden. The trees were thicker here, possibly self-sown from the woods beyond the fence, and the light was dimmer. Ralph's voice spoke behind me. 'It is there — to the left of that shrub,' he said. 'If the police can match that up with someone's coat, I think they will have the person they are looking for. I reckon it's . . . '

But his sentence was never finished. Afterwards, when Bill questioned me about it, I found it very difficult to remember what happened. I was bending over, searching for the tiny strand of tweed which Tennant said was there. I recalled a tiny sound, like a twig snapping perhaps as someone moved stealthily beneath the trees.

But I hardly noticed it for almost in the same second there was the noise of a shot. I whipped round. Ralph was bent nearly double, clutching his right arm with his left hand — and in obvious pain. But even as I ran towards him he straightened. 'Don't worry about me,' he called. 'I'll be all right. Go after them. Catch — whoever it was.'

I hesitated, wondering if I should insist on seeing to his injury first. But he was already pushing past me, tugging at the rusty wire, insisting that I should get under it. I scrambled down and through. He followed. We glanced to right and left among the trees but could see no one. Everything was quiet and unmoving.

'You go that way — I'll keep to the other side of the wood,' I whispered. He was still clutching his arm as he began to move quietly away in the direction I indicated.

And then, clear through the silence, from the pond on the far side of the trees, came a loud splash. Like a couple of machines, we both turned in the direction from which the sound had echoed. Ralph was slightly behind me when we reached the end of the wood. Walking quickly away from us, followed by a small brown dog was — Tiny Bullen.

'You stay here,' I ordered Ralph. 'I'll catch him up, insist he comes back to the bungalow with us. We can phone the police from there and tell them what has happened.'

Willingly he agreed and I saw him lean against a tree, his face white from shock and loss of blood.

'On second thoughts I think we will leave it to the inspector to do the arresting,' I stated. 'We both know exactly what occured and, if that splash was Tiny throwing the gun into the pool, the police will find it there. I'm sure I ought to get you back to the house and attend to that wound,' I told him.

Madeline came through from the passage as we stepped into the kitchen. Her face was as white as Tennant's when she caught sight of the two of us. 'What . . . what's happened?' she stammered.

'It's all right,' he assured her. 'Some fool tried to shoot me — but missed.'

'Missed!' She seemed unable to take her gaze from his arm.

'Oh, it's nothing,' he insisted, 'Just caught my arm a bit, that's all.' Then he crumpled to his knees.

I slipped my car keys out of my pocket and handed them to her. 'Please fetch my case from the car,' I said. She turned to carry out my request, but I could see she was very upset. Her hand trembled as she took the keys from me. I managed to get Ralph into a chair. Then I took off his jacket and pushed up the sleeve of his shirt.

It was not as bad as I expected. The bullet had gone right through his sleeve, grazing his arm. It was bleeding badly but would soon heal, I thought. He looked shaky, though. I went to his own room to fetch a tot of brandy.

'A few inches more and you would not have been so lucky,' I told him, handing him the glass.

He shuddered. 'Yes, I could easily have been the second victim,' he agreed, 'and I thought that Mr Rice was being a bit melodramatic yesterday. He will have to know about this.'

Before I could answer the door opened and Madeline came in with my case. She still looked white and shaken. 'When you have finished with me you had better do something for Madeline,' Tennant said, looking at her anxiously.

'Yes,' I agreed. 'Go on and lie down — try to relax,' I told her.

'But won't you want some help? Water . . . '

'No, I'll manage quite all right,' I said,

and she was too upset to insist on staying. I heard her go into her bedroom and close the door before I began to dress the wound. I had almost finished when Ralph said, 'Poor old Madeline — this is no help. I'll go and phone the police while you try to do something for her. Can you give her an injection perhaps to steady her?'

'I'll certainly give her a sedative,' I promised.

'I'm worried over her. She doesn't sleep or eat enough. For one thing she is fretting over the means to do up the bungalow . . . '

'Yes, she told me,' I replied.

'Did she now! Then perhaps it was you put her up to the idea of raising a mortgage on this place. I'm not sure it is a good idea, but if it is the only way for her to get some money — and it would set her mind at rest . . . '

'She had the idea before she talked to me,' I said. I had finished bandaging his arm. As I straightened he began to get to his feet, saying, 'Now you go and look at Madeline, while *I* phone the police.'

'Can you manage?' I asked, remembering how shaky he had been only minutes ago.

'I'm as fit as a fiddle now,' he said. 'I'll be all right.'

I found Madeline lying on her bed, covered with an eiderdown, but she sat up as I opened the door. She was in a highly nervous state and I realized that even with drugs and sedatives, it would be a long time before she recovered from the shock of her mother's death. It only needed something like today's occurence to upset her drastically. Yet perhaps that was natural. Someone had tried to shoot Ralph ... And then Madeline was putting into words something of what I was thinking.

'Whoever it was killed Mum — is out there — with a gun.' She was trembling, putting out her hand towards me, and I took it — trying to steady her with my own calm. 'I can't stay here,' she whispered. 'I just can't. Ian, take me away.'

And what else could I do? I think I took the only course possible. I said, 'I'll take you home with me. Miss Turner will look after you today.'

With agitated haste she began to get off the bed. 'I'll get my coat — shove some things in a case . . . You do mean I can stay at your house — overnight?'

'Yes. I'll go and wait for you out-side . . . '

'Don't leave me in this place alone.'

'I'll only be in the passage,' I promised.

I had been there no more than a moment or two when the connecting door opened and Ralph appeared. 'The inspector will be here as soon as possible,' he said.

'Well, until he comes take it easy,' I ordered, 'and I wouldn't let *anyone* in before he gets here . . . '

Madeline came out of her room behind me. 'Where are you going?' Tennant asked, surprise in his voice.

'I'm taking her back with me for a day or two,' I told him. 'She can't bear the idea of staying here — not after what has just happened — and I think it may do her good to have the company of another woman. Gwenda will be there . . . '

'How about me?' Ralph demanded. 'I've got to stick it out.'

'I'm sorry,' Madeline faltered, 'I'm sorry but . . . '

'All right,' he said. 'After all's said and done, I ought to be able to look after myself better than you can. But don't you think the inspector will want to see you too?'

'Tell him to come along to my house,' I replied.

Madeline did not speak as we drove through the dusking streets. When I had stopped outside my home and was helping her from the car I realized she was still very pale, and her arm was trembling as I held it to guide her along the path. When I opened the door Gwenda looked out of the dining room. Perhaps she had been going to say something about the meal for which I must be late. Instead she exclaimed, 'Madeline! Ian! What's wrong?'

I could not explain to her then, with Madeline at my side. I asked, 'Is the spare room bed made up?'

'Yes, and aired.'

'Then I think Madeline ought to go straight into it. She has had another shock. Do you mind helping her, Gwenda? I'll be up immediately.'

Later with Madeline safely in bed, I told Gwenda about the recent attack on Tennant and my sister said, 'Yes, I see that Madeline couldn't remain at the bungalow.' Yet I had the feeling that she did not want our one-time playfellow as a visitor in our home . . .

*   *   *

When Bill arrived some while afterwards Madeline was sound asleep. 'I gave her a sedative,' I said, 'and anyway, she could not help with this shooting affair. She was indoors all the time.'

'Are you sure of that?'

Well, was I? I didn't see her till I got back from the garden with Tennant. Inspector Gore had already been here and that was what I had had to admit to him.

'It looks rather as though she uses you, as her doctor, to form a buffer between herself and the questions the police want to ask her,' Bill said dryly, but I was glad that he did not pursue the matter any further. He made me give him an account of the affair in the garden of The Elms. Then he said, 'It's useless tonight because it's dark now — but I want you to come along tomorrow and reconstruct the shooting for me — just as it happened.'

'But there's nothing to reconstruct,' I protested. 'Surely Tennant can tell you as much as I can.'

'It was Tennant who got the bullet through his arm. I'd rather not worry him,' Bill said. 'When shall I come to pick you up?'

'I've got rather a full programme tomorrow,' I answered. 'It will have to be the afternoon.'

★ ★ ★

When Bill arrived he was carrying a parcel which he unwrapped. 'I borrowed the jacket Tennant was wearing at the time and I want you to put it on,' he said.

195

'You are about his height . . . '

'Is this really necessary?' I began, but suddenly Bill's face was more serious than I had ever known it.

'Ian, I don't need to remind you that we are investigating murder. I would not ask you to do this if it were *not* necessary.'

Without another word I took off my own jacket and put on Ralph's. It was a bit tight under the arms — he was slightly broader than me — but otherwise a good fit.

I slipped my coat on over it and went out to Bill's car. He slid into the driving seat and started the engine. As he edged the car out of our driveway I said, 'How about that splash we heard when we were in the wood yesterday?'

Glancing sideways at Bill I saw that he was smiling. 'You told me you thought the gun might be in the pond. You'd make a good detective. They dragged that pool and found all sorts of things — among them a weapon . . . '

'In that case it's pretty clear that Tiny Bullen fired it,' I said. 'There was no one else in the vicinity.'

Bill did not answer and I asked, 'By the way, did they find the strand of tweed Tennant had discovered on the wire? In the excitement I forgot all about it.'

Bill slowed the car a little as a lorry braked ahead of us. Then he said, 'All they found were one or two strands from the coat you were wearing and also one from Tennant's. You got under that wire more quickly than was good for your clothes!'

'I suppose we did. Our only thought was to catch the person who had fired the shot,' I admitted. 'But *I* saw the tweed that Ralph had found. It was from a dark blue coat.'

To my surprise Bill drove past the end of Rook Lane. 'I don't want anyone to watch our little reconstruction,' he said. 'If I stop my car outside The Elms, Tiny Bullen might be across to see what we are doing.'

'He has not been arrested yet?'

'No, and I asked him a few questions but he insists he was only out for a walk — that it was his dog rushing into the pond after a stone you heard.'

'But the gun! You say it was found in the water.'

'That is no *proof* of his guilt. Any fingerprints which might have been on it were effectively washed off. Neither you nor Tennant saw him throw it in. It may not even be *the* gun. We have yet to find the bullet which injured Ralph . . . '

We had reached the road which ran along the north side of the wood. Bill halted the car and we both climbed out, walking along the footpath which skirted the trees. The gardens of the houses in Rook Lane came down to this track, and most of them were tidy and well-kept. It would have been easy enough to find the weedgrown wilderness which belonged to The Elms, even if I had not known it. Bill quickly pulled up the wire for me to scramble under, as Ralph had done only yesterday. But *then* we had been coming out of the garden. Today Bill and I were crawling in.

He said, 'Will you stand in exactly the same position as Tennant was when he was shot?'

I looked around thoughtfully. Then I

took up my stance by a lilac tree — though 'tree' was rather a misnomer for it was a very thick bush. Untended for ages, it had grown in all directions, pushing out its roots until it claimed many square feet of soil.

'He was just here when I heard the shot and looked round to see him doubled up with pain,' I said.

'You are more sure about the position than he was,' Bill remarked.

'*I* hadn't been hit,' I replied. 'Poor old Ralph must have been pretty dazed for a few seconds.'

'Of course. Well, take off your coat for a minute.'

I did as he ordered, and Bill took a small round object from his pocket. It was one of those handy steel measures which carpenters use. He pulled it out to about a yard of its length and held it against the sleeve of the jacket I was wearing. The bullet holes, smudged with blood, where Tennant had held his arm after the shot, gaped up at me as I gazed at the ruler in Bill's hand.

'You see,' he said. 'This hole is where

the bullet entered the sleeve — and this is where it left. Does that convey anything to you?'

Seeing the steel measure held against the sleeve like that, it was quite obvious. 'The hole where the bullet *entered* is much higher than the other one,' I said.

'Exactly. So if we follow the line suggested by those two bullet holes, we might with luck find the bullet which caused them.'

He looked down ruefully at the weeds beneath our feet. 'Hopeless to think of finding anything at all there unless the search is carried out scientifically,' he said. 'I guess we can locate the bullet without much trouble, though — no more difficult, possibly, than dragging the pond to find the gun.' He stood deep in thought for several seconds. Then I saw him look up slowly, his eyes seeming to trace an invisible line from a point some distance beyond our feet, past those two bullet holes . . . up . . . up.

He moved, walked across to a tree just inside the fence — stood still and looked up into the branches. 'When you scrambled through this fence yesterday,' he said, 'you must have gone right under the person who fired that gun. The shot must have come from high up in this tree.'

I moved to his side. He was examining the tree trunk — and he was right. Here and there the bark had been kicked off. Someone had climbed up there — and the marks were very recent.

'What a fool I was!' I exclaimed. 'How the fellow must have laughed — sitting there in the dimness and watching us both racing away through the wood. Then climbing down and walking off quite slowly still laughing.'

'Man — or woman — up there, laughing?' Bill retorted. 'When the victim had escaped . . . '

'I see what you mean. Perhaps he didn't wait to see what happened to Ralph but was down that tree and away before we had time to collect our senses. But I don't remember hearing any noise — of cracking twigs, for instance, like I do recall from just before.'

'Or he could have leapt across the tree

tops and dropped down beside the pool before you reached it,' Bill said. He was still gazing up into the leafiness above him. There was an odd expression on his face.

'You mean — Tiny Bullen,' I averred.

'Perhaps.' He was smiling again, and I knew it would be useless to try persuading him to reveal his thoughts. All at once he said, 'Did you intend to see Tennant today?'

'About his arm? I told him to come to the surgery in a couple of days time. The wound was not very bad. I think he was suffering from shock mostly. If you think I ought to see him I will.'

'I do want to ask him a few more questions. Maybe it would be just as well if you were there.'

We went back to his car and, driving away from the wood, turned into Rook Lane. He said, 'I'll want to see Madeline too when I take you back.'

'All right — but be gentle with her,' I said. He didn't answer that. We were nearing The Elms and he told me, 'Don't mention the fact that we have been reconstructing the shooting — and keep your coat fastened, so that Tennant doesn't see you are wearing his jacket.'

Bill stopped his car but we had no chance to get out before Mrs Hodgson emerged through the gateway, carrying a basket. 'No good to go in there,' she said. 'Mr T.'s not in.' It was the first time I had heard her speak without being spoken to. Bill shrugged and drove on.

12

When we got back to my house Tennant was in the porch. He turned as we went up the path. 'I came to find out how Madeline is,' he said.

'You'd better come in,' I said and led the way towards our sitting room. Bill said, 'Perhaps Madeline will come and see you while I am here — I have come specially to interview her.'

'I expect she is still in her room,' I said. 'I'll send Miss Turner up to fetch her.'

If Madeline had looked ill yesterday she appeared ten times worse today. Perhaps it was partly because she was wearing no make-up, but there was no trace of colour in her cheeks, and even her lips were like a pale grey shadow.

'Come on in and sit down,' I said. 'Ralph has come to find out how you are.'

But she did not look at Tennant. Her glance had gone to Bill. 'Please don't worry — I only want to ask you a few simple questions,' he said.

She came reluctantly into the room and perched on the very edge of the settee. I saw Bill stroke his right eyebrow with one finger before he asked his first question. 'Did you know that Mr Tennant had found a small piece of tweed on the barbed wire at the bottom of your garden?'

She forced herself to look up at him but she did not speak.

'Well, did you? I just want you to answer yes or no.'

'Ye . . . es.' The answer came jerkily — as if dragged from her under torture.

'And did you pass on that information to anyone?'

Suddenly she turned away from him and buried her head in a cushion. Yet we only knew she was crying by an occasional heave of her shoulders. In all my experience as a doctor I had never known anyone cry so desperately or so silently before. I moved over to her and rested one hand on her shoulder. 'Please, Madeline,' I pleaded, 'please answer Mr

Rice because he is only trying to help you.'

'Help!' Ralph was beside her, pushing me away, and she turned to him, nuzzled her head into his shoulder. I saw him wince as she touched his bandaged arm. He looked up at us angrily. 'Can't you leave her alone, both of you. She's in no fit state to answer questions. You should know better than to allow it — you, a doctor.'

His anger seemed more directed at me than at Bill Rice. He looked down at Madeline. 'Let's get out of here,' he urged. 'Let me take you home.'

'No, no — I can't go back — there.'

Perhaps Bill thought it was hopeless. In any case, he began to move towards the door. 'I think it would be best if Miss Letts went back to bed and you gave her a sedative,' he said, looking at me. But there was no kindness in his voice. He was as angry in his way as Tennant, seeming unlike the Bill I knew.

But Ralph's anger had been because he wanted to protect someone he loved. My friend's was because he had failed to obtain the information he had been determined to get.

In the doorway he paused, and suddenly Madeline spoke. She was still leaning against Ralph but, though her face was streaked with tears, her sobs had ceased. 'I . . . I'm sorry I'm so . . . upset, Mr Rice,' she said. 'I . . . didn't want to get anyone into trouble — but Mr Bullen came over. He's . . . he's tried to get very friendly with Mrs Hodgson . . . like he did with . . . with my . . . mother . . . ' I saw her lean more heavily against Ralph and for a few moments I thought she was going to break down again.

'Yes?' Bill prompted.

'I . . . I was in my bedroom. I heard him trying to get Mrs Hodgson to talk . . . but she's not a very talkative person . . . '

She paused and again Bill had to prompt her before she said, 'He went on and on. I ought to have gone and told him to go away. If only I'd known . . . If . . . '

'If only you'd known what Miss Letts?'

'If only I'd known someone wanted to

kill Ralph I'd have done anything — *anything* to stop them.'

'We quite understand that, but will you please go on? You heard Mr Bullen trying to make Mrs Hodgson talk. Did she, in fact, say anything?'

'Yes. All at once she said, 'Mr Tennant thinks he knows who did the murder. He's found some evidence in the garden — so you can go and talk that over — with yourself'. I suppose she thought it would make him go and leave her in peace.'

I saw Bill's eyebrow's lift ever so slightly. 'So,' he said, 'Mrs Hodgson knew about the tweed on the wire.' And then, almost to himself, 'I don't suppose *she* would have a tweed coat.' The words were hardly above a whisper but Ralph obviously caught them.

'What the devil do you mean?' He demanded. 'Mrs Hodgson was right away from The Elms at the time of the murder — hadn't come to Mewsdale — she was an entire stranger to — to everyone.'

'At the moment I am investigating the shot which could have killed you, Mr

208

Tennant. That and Mrs Letts' death may — or may not — be connected.'

Madeline gave a convulsive shudder at the mention of her mother's name and started to get to her feet, but she swayed and would have fallen but for my arm. Ralph said gruffly, 'If you *won't* come home then I'll help you up the stairs.' And with his good arm he did just that.

I called Miss Turner to go and help, giving her two tablets to take up with her and telling her to give them to Madeline when she was settled into bed.

Bill's voice had been more kindly, I thought when, as Madeline passed him, he said, 'Thank you, Miss Letts. I'm sorry about all this, but believe me — it is necessary.'

'This affair has put her right back,' I remarked to him, but he did not seem to hear me.

'Are you coming round to The Elms to see this thing out?' he asked.

I hesitated. Then I said, 'Well, this is supposed to be my half-day. If you want my support . . . '

He was going on towards the front

door. Ralph came down the stairs. He passed me and followed Bill outside. 'I'll give you a lift back, Tennant — there are still a few points I want cleared up. You coming, Jax — you were there yesterday as well . . . '

I felt I would like to drive right away from all this miserable tragedy. Yet I found that I was going after the other two, getting into the back of Bill's car. Almost I expected Tennant to object to my presence, but he said nothing and, in fact, we did the short drive in complete silence.

We were in the sitting room at the front of The Elms — a room I was beginning to know quite well. Bill did not mention at once the subject which must have been upper-most in all our minds — the attack on Ralph. With his hands in his pockets, he stood and looked round him.

'I used to think once that I would like to be an explorer,' he said, 'and bring home trophies of my travels to hang up around the place like this. But it wasn't to be. I go hunting a different sort of game. Jove, these are some wonderful specimens!'

He walked over and gently touched the head of a deer before he moved on and looked up at a framed picture beside it. 'Splendid picture, that,' Ralph said from across the room. 'It's so typical of Africa. Kill or be killed is the unwritten law of the jungle. The tiger in that painting has claimed the life of an antelope, and the man in the background has shot the tiger.'

'I envy you your life of adventure,' Bill said.

'Yes, it holds plenty of excitement — yet there is something to be said for old England. One is glad to get back to civilization occasionally — although you could hardly call the things that have happened here recently civilized.'

'No I suppose not,' Bill agreed. 'Which brings us to the reason for my visit. Now, my belief is that the shot was fired at you, not from the wood, as you and the doctor imagined — but from the branches of a tree.'

Ralph was obviously startled. 'What

— goon would do that?' he demanded.

'A goon doesn't wait to shoot anybody,' Bill stated quietly. 'But whoever it was would hardly have waited indefinitely for days. It must have been someone who knew you might go along that path. Did you tell anyone that you were going to take the doctor into your confidence — and show him your 'evidence' that afternoon?'

'No.'

'But Mrs Hodgson knew you had found that bit of tweed — she as good as told Bullen about it — and Miss Letts overheard. I think I'd like to talk to Mrs Hodgson.'

'Dammit, man! I tell you, it was nothing to do with her. She was away all the afternoon.'

'Away . . . all . . . the . . . afternoon.' One by one Bill repeated the words, and suddenly the implication seemed to hit Ralph. I saw something leap into his eyes — an expression I could not define. He made no attempt to stop Bill when he crossed the room and called, 'Mrs Hodgson, will you come in here, please?'

She took her time answering the call but at last she came into the room. I glanced down at her feet as she shuffled across the carpet. They were encased in heavy shoes which were round-toed and flat-heeled — almost like a man's and as big.

She was a weird character. I wondered where Tennant had found her and if she, too, was involved in this affair as Bill appeared to think. Somehow I could not imagine *her* climbing trees. The thought amused me and yet, looking at her again, I was not sure. Shoes like that would be much easier for climbing than high-heeled ones — and her hands were rough and strong . . .

Bill's voice was saying, 'You had some time off yesterday, Mrs Hodgson. Do you mind telling me how you spent it?'

She gazed at him, aggressiveness in every line of her face.

'Well?' Bill pressed.

'Went to me sister,' she said then.

'And your sister's name and address?' He took out a notebook and scribbled down the particulars she gave him.

'Thank you. Now, where were you when Mr Tennant rang up the doctor and asked him to come here yesterday?'

'In the kitchen — I didn't listen to what he said.'

'No?' Bill paused. 'Mrs Hodgson, you knew the *real* reason why Mr Tennant wanted the doctor to come here.'

She did not answer. With her small dark eyes she glanced uneasily from Bill to Tennant, who said, 'Of course she didn't know — not until afterwards. Since I got shot there has been enough talk about that bit of tweed I found — but what happened to it? I suppose I should not have *left* it on the wire — then we'd still have the evidence . . . '

'I was trying to talk to Mrs Hodgson,' Bill said. 'Oh well, it doesn't matter. You can go,' he added to the woman.

She went off with her peculiar shambling gait and when she had shut the door behind her Bill said to Ralph, 'I guess we shall soon locate the person who fired that shot.' He began to move across the room and as I followed I told Tennant, 'I shall be taking surgery tomorrow evening.

214

You'd better come along then and let me dress that arm.'

He did not reply and I had the feeling he was still not very pleased with me. In a way I could understand him. He had discovered what he thought would be important evidence and, because of that discovery, he had escaped death by inches. Not only that, but the shooting incident had meant more distress and unhappiness for Madeline — and resulted in her leaving the bungalow . . .

Bill turned in the doorway. 'I advise you not to leave the house for a day or two, Mr Tennant. I'm sure the police will send a man along to keep an eye on it from the outside. Next time you might not be so lucky . . . as I think Inspector Gore will agree.'

'If the police had done their job properly it would never have happened. *They* are doing the investigating. They should have discovered that fragment of tweed.'

We were in the hall now and Bill had opened the door. As he stepped outside I followed him, and Ralph closed the door behind us before Bill could reply.

We went silently back to the car. We neither of us spoke till we reached the end of Rook Lane, and then Bill said, 'We reconstructed the shooting except for the actual time. When did it happen?'

'Not long before Tennant phoned Gore,' I told him. 'I arrived at the bungalow about quarter to five. I remember glancing at my watch as I got out of my car and thinking I was early. Indeed Ralph remarked on that fact as I met him coming round from the back. I had told him I would be there at five.'

'Did you go into the house and see Madeline Letts before you went into the garden?'

'No, I suppose Ralph was afraid it would get too dark if we didn't go straight away.'

'So, by the time you reached the bottom of the garden and the shot was fired it would have been, say, ten minutes to five?'

'Yes, about that.'

'Then you ran through the wood, saw Mr Bullen and then came straight back to the bungalow . . . When you reached it the time could have been ten past . . . quarter past five?'

I was beginning to get almost as tired of his questions as Ralph had been, and was glad we were nearly back at Roseville. I agreed wearily, 'Yes, I suppose it would have been about quarter past. I dressed his wound . . . '

'Why didn't you ring *me* directly you got within reach of a phone? That would have given me a chance to get there in daylight.'

'Bill, I am a doctor. Ralph was in a pretty poor way — I had to see to him. Then Madeline was in a state of collapse. I went to look after her while Ralph phoned Gore up. In fact she was almost in a worse condition than he was. It must have been an awful shock to her, seeing us come in like that, with Ralph in such obvious pain and his clothes smothered in blood.'

'That reminds me,' Bill said. 'You still have his jacket on! I'll wait while you take it off.'

He drew to a halt outside my gate. 'I

won't come in,' he said. 'You can take the coat off here in the car.'

Obediently I wriggled out of my own overcoat and then Tennant's jacket, folding it and turning to put it on the back seat of the car. 'Sorry I've taken up so much of your half-day,' Bill apologized.

'That's all right,' I returned, but with relief I got out of his car. This had been anything but a pleasant afternoon.

13

I was approaching the entrance to Pine's Cutting the next morning when out of the narrow right-of-way shot a black cat, followed closely by a brown dog. A quickly-moving figure emerged just behind the animals, and I could not resist a chuckle at the ridiculous sight of Tiny Bullen — so tall and long-legged in pursuit of his dachshund, which was so short-legged and long — in the opposite direction.

My call was at a house near-by and as I got out of my car I saw that Tiny had come to a halt outside the garden next door. At the foot of a tree crouched Rocket, barking furiously. The cat had taken refuge high in the branches of an oak tree.

'Oh dear,' Tiny remarked, glancing towards me. 'Rocket has chased a cat up there . . . '

'I wouldn't worry,' I said. 'Once you

have taken your dog away the cat will come down. Cats can look after themselves.'

'I suppose so. Come on, Rocket.' The dog obeyed reluctantly, but before I was admitted to my patient's house he and his master had disappeared from view.

It was a stupid little incident which I should have forgotten — except for what ensued the next morning. Then I was called out early to the old man I had been visiting when I met Bullen the day before — and I saw him again.

Which sight of him I could *not* forget. I made it my business to go round to Bill's hotel later on and what I was hoping for proved to be fact — my friend's car was outside. Stopping my own Consul, I got out. Minutes later Bill was admitting me to his large room. He gestured to one of the deep leather armchairs and, when I was seated, took his place opposite me.

'Why the serious face?' he demanded.

'It's about Tiny Bullen — do you remember I said that Gore asked him why *he* had not climbed in the window to go to Mrs Letts' rescue?'

'Yes, he implied he was too old and creaking-jointed, I believe.'

'Which I have discovered is far from true,' I stated quietly. 'Yesterday morning I saw him sprinting along like a man less than half his age. But that didn't strike me at all at the time. It was this morning which set me thinking. Yesterday his dog chased a cat up a tree. Today the thing was still there. I heard it miaow as I got out of my car. But before that I had seen Tiny Bullen on the ground beneath the tree. I was in a hurry, because I had been called urgently, but as I went up the path to my patient's house Tiny was nowhere to be seen. The cat was still crying . . . '

'Yes?' Bill was still smiling. Perhaps he thought my story fatuous, but I ploughed on, 'Well, not long afterwards, from my patient's window upstairs I saw Bullen. He dropped down from among the leaves of the lowest branch of that oak — and he was holding the black cat. Listen, Bill — he had been right to the top of that tall tree. Not agile! He could have climbed

221

through the Letts' window more easily than Charlie Herbert could. For one thing, he is a good bit thinner than Charlie . . . '

'And so you suggest?'

'That Tiny Bullen *knew* Mrs Letts was inside that door — probably knew she was murdered and was not prepared to go into that kitchen alone . . . '

'Why not alone? He went in with Nurse Mackail.'

'If . . . if . . . ' But I could not go on with what was in my mind. To accuse a fellow-human of cold-blooded murder was rather horrible. I added quickly, 'Someone climbed that tree in the garden the other day. Now we know it *could* have been Tiny.'

Bill said, '*You* have it in your mind that Bullen is the man I want — yet you have just told me he would risk his neck climbing a tree to rescue a *cat*. And I know he is an animal lover. Didn't *you* see the way he fondled the head of his dachshund when we went there. Bullen is essentially a *gentle* man.'

'With *animals*,' I replied, 'but people's

attitudes differ, even where creatures are concerned.'

I glanced at Bill. He did not look amused now, and I went on, 'Take a farmer, for instance. He'll think the world of his dog — but brag that it is a ratter. Well, the *rats* are animals. They squeal when caught and so they must have feelings — but does the farmer consider that aspect of the matter?'

'*Can* you compare dogs with vermin?' Bill asked.

'To some humans other humans might be vermin,' I retorted.

'You don't suggest that Mrs Letts appeared in that light to Mr Bullen?'

'No — I don't suppose so,' I had to admit.

'He apparently wanted to marry her, you know,' Bill remarked.

'Oh, you know that?' I asked and Bill smiled.

'It's my business to know as much as I can about my suspects . . . '

'Then you concede Bullen *is* that,' I put in.

'So are several others,' Bill told me

laconically, 'though I think I have eliminated a couple of my first firm favourites . . . '

'Tell me,' I began but he shook his head. 'Not yet,' he said. 'I have to be *sure* before I make a move.'

'Well, here's something you *can* be sure of,' I said. 'Of all your suspects Tiny Bullen must be the one most used to death. He has lived with it as his profession almost all his life.'

'Um . . . yes . . . ' Bill agreed thoughtfully.

I said, 'By the way, you promised to let me know if you managed to find out anything about John Harvey — you know, whether he did *not* go on that train, as I suggested.'

'I was going to tell you. Your guess was right. He went back to London in the early hours of the morning — cadged a lift from a lorry driver — nor was it the first time he had done it, either.'

'So he could have been coming here before . . . To see Mrs Letts? Or Madeline?' I suggested. 'That afternoon I went there to see Tennant she appeared very friendly with him.'

'But according to your account of what happened he didn't know her name was Letts.'

'No . . . o . . . o,' I confessed. 'No, the name seemed to come as a surprise to him that afternoon.'

Bill said, 'Nurse Mackail came to me with her news a little late — *she* had discovered that he did not take the train he averred back to town — she came to tell me so yesterday.'

'Did she now! So, though she has been about a lot with Harvey, it has not been as a friend. She is obviously trying to implicate him. Because, now it is known he did not leave on that train, then he could have returned to The Elms. But with what motive?'

'That's just it. Have you any suggestion?' Bill asked.

'No — but something else occurs to me. That evening, when Tiny Bullen went over there and Mrs Letts was so keen to get rid of him apparently — there could have been someone in the place — someone who did not want to be seen . . . '

'Who?'

'I wish I knew,' I said. 'Bill, this affair is beginning to get on top of me. *Can't* you put your hand on anyone?'

'Why should it be getting you down so much? Because you are afraid — because you can't forget that Gwenda went to The Elms that night?' Bill demanded in a quiet tone. Despite anything my sister might say, he was sure she had gone there *and*, I had to admit to myself, so was I . . .

Suddenly I knew I couldn't just remain idly waiting any longer. I had to *do* something, and soon. The next day I was in my car heading north.

I put my foot hard down on the accelerator, feeling glad in a way that I should soon reach the end of my journey. Only another three miles and I should be in Cleand, the town where Gwenda had worked for quite a while. What had happened to my sister in this place to change her from the happy companion she had once been into the secretive, unhappy woman she was now?

I was determined to find out although I

almost despised myself for that determination. It seemed so much like spying. And yet it was because of Gwenda's own deception that I was deceiving her now and I was doing it, I believed, for her own happiness. If I could discover what sort of cloud overshadowed her past, perhaps I could help to disperse it.

I reached the outskirts of the town and drew the car to a halt opposite a small restaurant. It was early afternoon, too late for lunch yet much too soon for tea, and there were only one or two other customers. I did not feel like much to eat and ordered beans on toast and a pot of tea.

As the waitress put my plate in front of me I asked if she could tell me how to find Camel Street. Following her directions a short while later, I discovered it without difficulty. Within a few minutes I was ringing the bell at Number Twenty-one. There was a pause before the door opened to reveal a tall aggressive-looking woman in a dark blue overall which seemed to reach from her neck to her ankles.

She snapped out a curt, 'Well?' before I had time to say, 'Good afternoon.'

'I wanted to make a few enquiries,' I said at last.

'Then it's the information bureau you want,' she snapped again, starting to close the door in my face.

As quickly as the most experienced commercial traveller, I put my foot into the narrowing gap. 'I'm sorry — I know your time is valuable but, please, this is important.'

'I'm sure — important that I should use your spin drier or sewing machine or other high falutin' gadget, I suppose. Well, I'm not interested.'

'I am not selling anything,' I stated firmly. 'I simply want to ask about a young lady who used to live here.'

'Then you can take yourself off just the same. We do not give information about our young ladies to *anyone*, no matter how respectable they *look*.' For a second I was amused at the image of myself as a wolf in sheep's clothing, but the next moment I remembered why I was here on this doorstep, pleading with this guardian of 21 Camel Street. I had come for Gwenda's sake. I grew suddenly desperate. I thrust my hand into my pocket and withdrew the photo, picked up that morning in the Letts' bungalow. I thrust it in front of the woman.

'That's a picture of my sister,' I said. 'I just want to know where she used to work.'

She glanced at the square of paper and I saw recognition leap into her eyes, but she wasn't looking at Gwenda. She said, 'We don't ask where our residents work. It's no concern of ours. But I daresay *everybody* knows *he* worked at Greets.'

I had taken my foot from the doorway and suddenly the door slammed shut. The dragon was determined not to waste any more time on me. I stood there feeling dazed and puzzled, still holding the photograph in my hand. I looked again at the man's smiling face and once more the feeling of having seen him, of knowing him, came back to me. Perhaps, I thought, it is some sort of telepathy. Gwenda knew him — had loved him enough to marry him. Perhaps, because he still exists in her mind so clearly, his image has been transfered to mine by some sort of telepathic process . . .

Because he exists in her mind . . . but does he exist in reality? Was he now dead or had they just separated when they discovered that their marriage was not a success? But if that was it, why couldn't she have told me?

I replaced the photograph in my pocket, and went back to my car. If I had not actually discovered where Gwenda worked, at least I had some sort of lead — Greet's. It was not a name she had ever mentioned — but then she had never talked about her employers . . .

I stopped by the next telephone kiosk and looked up the name in a directory. Greet Electra Company . . . That must be it. I jotted down the address on a scrap of paper.

It turned out to be a huge building, about fifteen stories high, and I felt very small as I went up wide stone steps and in at a revolving door.

The heat of the place seemed almost to strike me after the cold wind outside. I was in a huge foyer, with doors on every side and a carpeted stairway leading up from the further side of it. There was a desk near the foot of the stairs, but it was unoccupied. I moved slowly across the intervening space, uncertain what I should do. Somehow I had expected to find someone who would direct me to the manager's office, but the place was completely deserted.

I stood for a while looking down at the desk-top, wondering if there might be a bell which should be rung for attention. But there was not and I decided, if no one arrived within a few minutes, I would knock on one of the doors. It seemed strange that the place was so quiet — no sound even of a typewriter. I thought how easy it would be for anyone to walk right through the building unnoticed. Perhaps it did not matter that access was so simple — if this was just a block of offices, with nothing of value in any of them . . .

Impatiently I turned to approach the nearest door and had almost reached it when it opened and a young woman came towards me. 'You wanted something?' she asked, looking at me from beneath well-arched eyebrows.

'I should like to see Mr Greet.'

She slid down on to the chair behind the desk and her eyebrows arched even higher.

'Mr Greet? You did say Mr Greet . . . '

'He's the manager, isn't he?'

'Managing Director he was — but not any more. It's Mr Guest now. Mr Greet is dead — stone cold by now, I reckon.'

She spoke insolently, and I felt annoyed. I thought I should get no more information from this modern miss than I had from the landlady in Camel Street. I said, 'I am trying to trace a Miss Gwenda Jax who, I believe, may have worked here.' I paused, meeting the girl's impudent gaze, and adding quickly, 'I . . . I'm a solicitor and I hold some information which will be to her advantage.'

I don't know why the lie leapt to my lips so readily. I was surprised to hear myself telling it — almost it seemed as if someone else had spoken the words for me.

The insolent expression vanished, and

the girl's face softened as I mentioned Gwenda's name. 'Gwenda Jax,' she repeated softly. 'She used to be Mr Greet's secretary. We all liked Gwenda. I have to see everyone clocks in and clocks out at the right time. Gwenda always had a bright smile when she arrived in the morning. She left here, though. I don't know where she's working now. If you want to find her because of a legacy or something I wish I could help you — I'd willingly do anything for Gwenda.'

She paused. '*Has* she been left some money?'

It was a cue I could follow. 'It depends on if Miss Jax had married or not as to whether she can claim it,' I said. 'Do *you* know if she is married?'

'No, no, not when she was here, anyway. Some folks said she went around a lot with — James Royce, but I don't think it was true.'

There had been a fraction of a pause before the name and I wondered why. James Royce — the name was vaguely familiar — like the photograph I carried in my pocket. For the second time that day I took it out and held it for someone to see.

I was astonished at the way the girl's face changed again. The old, insolent look returned — but now it was accompanied by defiance. 'You lied,' she almost shouted at me. 'You don't want to help Gwenda. You are here to ask more questions about — that fellow. Well, I won't tell you anything. The management instructed us we were to say nothing about it at the time, and I won't now.'

'It is the Managing Director I want to see,' I reminded her.

'Well, you can't then. He's at a board meeting this afternoon. Besides, he never sees anyone without an appointment.' She opened a large, important-looking ledger on the desk and began to write. I was dismissed. Should I try and make an appointment for another day?

But how would it help if I did? If this girl knew Gwenda quite well and yet did not know about her marriage, would someone who had taken over since Gwenda worked here be able to help?

Slowly I walked back across the carpet

to the door. There seemed no point in staying any longer in Cleand. I went back to my car and began the long drive home. What had I achieved by this attempted detective work of mine? Nothing at all which would help Gwenda. I had merely succeeded in getting myself more tangled up than before.

I kept remembering the things the girl at Greet's had said. 'The management instructed us *at the time* . . . ' What time? 'You are here to ask more questions about *that fellow* . . . ' The man whose photograph was in my pocket and who had, seemingly, married Gwenda? Was he James Royce?

It was raining now and I switched on the windscreen wiper. With every click of it, as it swung across and back again, the name seemed to repeat. James . . . Royce . . . James . . . Royce . . . James . . . And then Gwenda's name was there too — both of them synchronised with the rhythm of the tapping gadget. Gwen-da . . . James-Royce . . . Gwen-da.

I felt I could stand it no longer. I drew the car to the side of the road and switched off the engine. Resting my hands on the steering wheel, I gazed at the rain-drenched road ahead.

I knew that I could not go on like this. All that had happened during the past weeks had worn me down until I was becoming a nervous wreck — tormented by the tapping of a windscreen wiper, which I had heard a million times before and never noticed. I had to do *something* — but what?

My efforts as a detective had not got me far. 'A ruddy detective' — that's what John Harvey had said. He was right, too. And I had advised *him* to take the police into his confidence — something I had not been prepared to do myself.

In the first place it had been wrong for me to take that photograph — perhaps it was even a criminal offence. It was not even as though I did not know Bill. Suddenly my mind was made up. I would go to *him* now — put all my cards on the table and let him take over the hand. I had been playing solo far too long where this photo business was concerned. I reached The Lion just as he was leaving it.

'Gosh, Ian!' he exclaimed when he saw me. 'You look just about all-in. What's the matter?'

'I'd like a chat with you,' I said. 'Can we go somewhere that we won't be interrupted?'

'I was just on my way out,' he said. 'But come on back to my room and have a drink.'

Gratefully I excepted that invitation — a drink was just what I needed.

Sitting in his large hotel room a few minutes later, a glass of whisky in front of me, I wondered how to begin.

'Come on, Ian,' he urged. 'Something has been worrying you lately. What is it? To do with our murder case, I'd bet . . .'

'The fact is,' I admitted, 'I have been keeping something from you . . .'

'Suppressing evidence.' He grinned but I did not return the smile.

'You see,' I said, 'I think Gwenda *is* mixed up in it somehow and I have been trying to do a little sleuthing on my own today — but it hasn't worked out.'

'*Gwenda* mixed up in it! What gives you that idea?' He scratched one eyebrow with a well-manicured pudgy finger, and I felt that he was being a trifle sarcastic. *He* knew she had gone to the bungalow that evening.

'This,' I said, producing the photograph and putting it down on a small table between us. I was beginning to hate that small print, to feel that I should like to toss it into the fire and watch it crumble to ash. Which was what Gwenda had wanted me to do in the beginning . . . Her voice echoed now in my ears — 'Destroy it — not only for *my* sake . . . ' And inwardly I begged, 'Gwenda, forgive me.'

Bill picked up the small photograph — looked at it. I saw his lips tighten into a firm, straight line. It seemed an eternity before he spoke. Then he said the most unexpected thing. His words hung in the room with us long after he had spoken them. 'Are you sure,' he asked, 'that this is Gwenda?'

I took it from him and studied it again. 'Of course I'm sure,' I insisted.

'But it is a wedding picture. Did you know she was married?'

'No.'

'Does your father know?'

'I'm sure he doesn't.'

'And you haven't shown him this?'

'No,' I said, 'I wanted to discover the secret behind it before I confided in anyone. After all, it is really Gwenda's secret. I tried to get her to tell me about it but she refused. I have tried to play the detective because I wanted to help her.'

'Then keep her secret for a little while longer, Ian,' Bill said. 'Let me have this photograph. I promise you I'll do nothing to hurt your sister. Do not tell her — or anyone else — that you have given me this. You see, I know who this man is . . . '

I wanted to ask if it was James Royce but, somehow, I did not have the courage. Something about the look in his eyes, the set of his mouth, warned me it would be better if I did not know.

He reached across and took the photo from me again. 'By the way,' he said, 'you did not tell me where you got it.'

I had begun this thing — I had to tell the truth now.

'It must have been there — under Mrs Letts' body all night,' I finished.

'And that makes you think Gwenda is mixed up in the murder,' he said. 'Well, *I* don't think she is. Go home and forget all about this, Ian. And leave the detective work to me.'

He had not asked me what I meant when I said I had been doing some sleuthing on my own account. Almost, in my relief at sharing my anxieties, I had forgotten it myself.

In a few words I related the way I had spent my afternoon. 'Don't tell Gwenda you have been to Cleand,' he counselled. 'I am your friend, Ian. Please do as I say and try to forget you have ever seen this small oblong of paper.' And then slowly, 'I think possibly you have helped to solve two murders.'

'*Two* murders? You mean one and an attempt . . . '

He shook his head but he made no further explanation. He picked up his glass and drained it to the last drop. 'If I were you I'd go to bed early tonight,' he said. 'You look as if you need a few hours of solid sleep.'

I stood up. 'I feel a lot less worried now I have talked to you,' I admitted. 'I think I *shall* sleep better tonight.'

14

It was true what I had said to Bill — I felt better after shifting my worry off on to his shoulders, but my anxiety had changed to a sense of impending climax. I was waiting for something to happen — but it did not immediately.

Tennant came to my surgery — his wound was healing nicely. He saw Madeline briefly but, though she was considerably better, she refused to go home. 'Because she knows you are soft and will be prepared to let her stay here indefinitely,' Gwenda said to me irritably.

I had thought it might help both the girls for them to get together — but it was not working out that way. The atmosphere in our home was even more electrically tense. On the Friday morning I could feel it as something almost tangible. What had I started when I took pity on Madeline?

One of my calls that afternoon took me

near the river and I felt a sudden urge to hear its soothing purl, so instead of getting into my car after seeing my patient, I went down to the water's edge.

I stood on the bank, just below the bridge. Through one of its arches I could see across to the further brink of the river — the meadow with its one solitary horse, the path frequented at weekends by fishermen . . . Today on that path were two figures that I recognised — Nurse Mackail and Ralph Tennant. I saw the woman put out her hand to Ralph and he took it. Then he turned abruptly away. She took a step or two after him, flinging out her arms — almost as though pleading with him, but if she said anything he took no notice. I saw him stride away from her. I thought there was an impatient lift to his shoulders — or did I imagine that?

When at last I moved to go back to my car Nurse Mackail was still there on the path at the far side of the river.

Impatient? If I had only fancied that in Ralph, I knew it was the feeling in my own heart. I drove round by The Lion

Hotel . . . I had to see Bill — to ask him if he had made any progress in his enquiries. No good to tell me to forget — how could he *expect* me to do that?

I was pleased to find he was in his room. He looked up at me when I went in, after tapping on his door. 'Well, any more vital evidence to give me?' he chaffed.

'No, but I have just seen Nurse Mackail and Tennant,' I told him and described the little tableau I had just witnessed.

'Of course I couldn't hear what they were saying,' I remarked. 'It was like watching a ballet — all in mime, but I didn't have any book of words to tell me the story, so I couldn't interpret the little drama. Anyway, I don't suppose it would help if I'd heard every word they had said. I keep telling you what seem to be unimportant, disconnected scraps . . . '

'Ah, but *is* this one unconnected?' he mused. 'Remember you saw Nurse Mackail with John Harvey. I have a feeling I must get a move-on — or there really will be another murder . . . '

That was Friday. On Saturday I woke

with Bill's statement still ringing in my ears.

When I went along to the bathroom for my shave I could hear voices coming from the spare room — Gwenda was in there with Madeline. I did not catch any word yet somehow as I went on and picked up my razor I had an uneasy feeling. Why? Simply because my sister was talking to Madeline Letts quite early in the morning? Because it *was* early. Gwenda did not have to go to the office today and usually indulged in the luxury of a lie in.

There was no tray ready for Madeline's breakfast when I got down that morning. I suppose Gwenda saw that I missed it. She said, 'I don't see why I or Miss Turner should wait on that girl. She is playing on your sympathy, Ian. *She* isn't the only one to lose a mother in tragic circumstances, but other folk have to keep a stiff upper lip.'

Gwenda picked up the teapot. 'She ought to pull herself together. I've told her she must come down to breakfast this morning.'

But Madeline did not appear, and that

odd feeling of uneasiness was intensified for me. I pushed back my plate after finishing my bacon and eggs, put a piece of toast on my smaller plate. But before spreading it with marmalade I got to my feet. 'Where are you going?' Gwenda demanded.

'To tell Madeline breakfast is ready.'

My sister did not reply, but I could feel her anger.

I went upstairs, knocked on the door of the spare room. There was no reply.

Not many minutes later I was back in the dining room. 'Madeline is not in the house,' I announced.

I could see that Gwenda was taken aback. She began, 'Well . . . '

But a ring at the doorbell interrupted her. I went myself to answer it. Bill was outside. 'You are here early,' I said inadequately. 'We are just feeling a bit . . . ' I broke off. I did not know quite what I felt. I said after a moment, 'Madeline is gone.'

'What do you mean? She didn't sleep here?' I thought there was an edge to Bill's voice.

'No — she must have left here not long ago. She hasn't had her breakfast . . . '

'I guess she's gone back to The Elms.' That was Gwenda's voice behind me.

Back to that place she dreaded — because my own sister had made her feel unwelcome here . . .

Bill was saying, 'Oh lor! Hurry . . . I'd come to ask you two to go to Rook Lane with me. Now there is need for haste. I don't want matters precipitated. Come on — both of you.'

I saw that Gwenda wanted to refuse to go — but she did not.

And as for myself . . . Well, there were my patients to consider. Bill urged, 'Ian, you must come.' And I, too, felt compelled by his insistent urgency. I rushed upstairs to tell Dad *he* would have to take the morning surgery and, if I was not back, start the round.

When I got back Gwenda was already in Bill's car, which he had started before I got in. He was off and with a jerk I fell on to the seat. We had gone some yards before I could slam the door shut.

As we passed Nurse Mackail's home I

caught the glimpse of a plain clothes man in her garden. She had obviously been under observation all night.

We reached The Elms. Bill rang the front door bell but did not wait to be answered. He entered the hall, went towards Ralph's sitting room. Gwenda, just ahead of me, was obviously reluctant to go inside.

Glancing beyond her, I halted suddenly — the hall was strangely empty. Alligators, leopard skin and assegais were all gone.

The door half-way along the passage opened slowly. Bill's hand outstretched towards the sitting room door handle, paused. He swung round. He breathed a sigh of relief when he saw Ralph standing in the doorway. 'Thank goodness!' he exclaimed. 'I came as quickly as I could, Mr Tennant, but I was afraid I might be too late.'

'Thank you,' Ralph said, 'but I can't admit to much faith in you or the police. There has been a constable stationed outside the bungalow but what sort of protection is that? One man to protect someone who has already been almost murdered.'

He moved towards us and I could see the troubled expression in his eyes. 'When I came back to England after my last safari, I booked a return passage for this month,' he went on. 'Then I decided, when I found a comfortable home here, that I would cancel my booking and stay in the old country for a while. I have made up my mind *now* I will go on the trip after all. Perhaps I shall be safer in an African jungle than I am in England. At least one *knows* the dangers there and can prepare for them.'

As he spoke he moved across to open the sitting room door. I made to follow him and was suddenly gazing at the most weird scene I have ever witnessed in my life.

In the middle of the floor John Harvey was kneeling beside a large packing case. He was surrounded by crocodiles, all sorts of spears and native weapons, and glass cases containing birds and fish. Animal heads lay on the thick carpet and snarled up at the ceiling above them.

Bill said, 'Good morning, Mr Harvey.' The man was placing a particularly ferocious-looking lion's head in the packing case, and he finished lowering the thing carefully into position before he got slowly to his feet. 'Mr Rice!' he said. 'I did not expect to see *you* here this morning.'

'I'm afraid I cannot return the compliment — if that is the right expression,' Bill returned, 'for I *did* expect to find *you* here.'

Harvey scowled but he did not reply and into the silence Ralph Tennant said, 'John will look after my souvenirs while I am away. I must be sure I leave them in good hands — they have a certain sentimental value for me.'

It seemed almost macabre to me, linking sentiment with animals one had deprived of life, but Ralph was obviously sincere. *I* have never been able to understand the hunter's outlook — it is so very different from that of a doctor whose whole instinct is, not to destroy, but to save life.

Suddenly Bill swung round and then I saw Madeline. She was slumped in a corner of the settee. I glanced at Bill, but his expression betrayed nothing. He was moving towards the girl and she looked up at him, eyes wide and startingly blue against the dead-white of her face.

All at once I realised that Gwenda had not followed me into the room and I turned back to the hall. She was just outside the door — leaning back against it. 'Why has he made us come here — why?' she demanded, her voice low and frightened.

I slipped an arm round her shoulder. 'Gwenda,' I said, 'look at me.' She did as I commanded, and in her expression I could see the shadow and fear which now seemed almost part of her. I said, 'You won't confide in me, Gwenda, but you are afraid. When we are scared of anything it is best to go right up to it — not to run away. Then often, we are not fearful any more.'

'All right, I'll try to do what you say,' she whispered and moved out of my encircling arm. I followed her into the sitting room. I noticed that as she went she was nervously twisting and untwisting her gloves between her hands.

As we went in Bill glanced round at us. He said, 'Mr Harvey is packing up. He came down by train last evening. He doesn't *always* come — or go by train.'

Abruptly Harvey sat back on his heels, apparently startled.

'You seem very knowledgeable about John's affairs.' It was Madeline's voice which interrupted him, and I saw Gwenda glance at the other girl and then look quickly away.

'It is my business to be knowledgeable about people's affairs,' he said. 'It is really surprising how much I know about all sorts of things.'

'Then perhaps you know we are busy,' John Harvey put in. 'I don't suppose it is me you have come to see, but whoever it is, please make it short. Mr Tennant, too, has no time to spare.'

'As a matter of fact I *have* come to see you — *and* a lot of other folk . . . ' Bill paused, glancing down at the littered carpet and then saying, 'Would it take very long to move these creatures to one side? This is the largest and most convenient room in the bungalow and I want space to arrange a few chairs.' He stooped over and picked up one of the native spears, balancing it carefully on one finger and letting it fall again as he spoke. It hit the floor with a small thud and Gwenda, standing close beside me, jumped.

John Harvey protested, 'All this has to be packed.'

'I appreciate that, Mr Harvey, but I have something to tell you — something more important than your packing.'

There was a ring on the door bell and Mrs Hodgson shuffled through the hall to answer it.

'Ah, Mr Bullen — I thought you would be dropping in,' Bill said as Tiny appeared in the doorway. Bill glanced quickly round at us. 'I think we are all here now except Nurse Mackail. And she should not be very long. I phoned her earlier to say her services might be required here this morning. Well, shall we all help to move these things out of the way while we are waiting . . . '

'Waiting for what?' Madeline's voice

startled us. I had, myself, almost forgotten she was there.

'For Nurse Mackail of course. When she arrives our circle will be almost complete,' Bill replied, picking up a tiger's head as he spoke and placing it carefully on the window sill. John Harvey made an attempt to protest, but I did not hear what Bill said, for Gwenda was tugging at my sleeve. For a moment I thought she was going to turn and dash out of the room. I put out my hand and squeezed hers, and was glad to see the panic gradually evaporate from her eyes. But she made no attempt to help move the many trophies. Tiny Bullen did most of that, giving a strange sort of running commentary as he worked, and interrupted once or twice by angry grunts from Harvey.

When it was finished Bill said, 'That's fine. Now will you all sit down? You in the chair by the window, Miss Jax, and perhaps you will sit by your sister, Dr Jax. You, Mr Tennant, can share the settee with Miss Letts. Mr Harvey will take the chair next to it.'

Why did we all so meekly obey? I can only speak for myself, but all at once Bill had ceased to be anything except a very real detective with the indisputable authority denoted by that title. He was standing to watch us carry out his orders. We were hardly seated when the door bell rang and, seconds later, Mrs Hodgson opened the door to announce, 'Nurse Mackail.'

'Ah, come right in,' Bill said. 'And you too, Mrs Hodgson.' He pointed to two chairs on the opposite side of the window from where I sat with Gwenda.

The nurse seemed confused to see us all. 'I thought . . . ' she began. 'I thought that you . . . '

'Yes, I told you someone might need your services. Well, so they may later but meanwhile I want you here the same time as these other people.'

Mrs Hodgson had begun to go out of the room, closing the door behind her, but Bill's voice reached her. 'No, come back,' he called imperiously, and slowly she reopened the door. Reluctantly she shuffled into the room. The nurse was already in the chair Bill had indicated, and very slowly Mrs Hodgson went to sit beside her.

For some moments there was silence, broken only by the tick of a clock in a carved mahogany case on the mantel-piece. Gwenda was still twisting and untwisting the gloves which she held in her hands. Madeline sat hunched up, arms tightly folded, a defiant expression now on her face.

Bill had taken up his own stance not far from the door.

John Harvey, still angry at being halted in the middle of his task, lay back in his armchair, his hands thrust deep into his pockets. Ralph Tennant, in his corner of the settee, was holding the mounted head of an antelope — once long ago it had been a beautiful creature. He was gently stroking it — it might have been a favourite dog whose ears he was fondling.

After what seemed an eternity Bill Rice began to speak, and everyone glanced up at him. Everyone, that is, except Gwenda who went on looking at her gloves and twisting them finger by finger — and John

Harvey who was looking at a picture on the opposite wall.

Bill's voice stated, 'You are all here this morning for a reason. A short while ago an old lady was murdered in this bungalow. One of you murdered her.'

I glanced quickly round at the other faces. Mrs Hodgson looked sulky, Nurse Mackail hautily aloof. If John Harvey and Ralph Tennant registered anything in their expressions, it was impatience. And Madeline . . . My gaze halted longer on her. She was made-up but I realized that, beneath the false eye lashes, her eyes were red-rimmed — and I felt suddenly angry with Bill that he was subjecting her to this. It was distressing to lose one's parent in any circumstance — I knew that keenly enough. My own loss had been harassing, but to find one's mother had been brutally murdered . . .

And then be subjected to a host of questions — to be sitting here in a room like this, having been told that the person who had committed the terrible crime was here as well . . .

I was suddenly aware that Bill was

talking to Gwenda. '*You* came to the bungalow on the evening of Mrs Letts' murder. It is useless to deny it — I have proof that you did.'

Gwenda looked up. Her glance went straight to Tiny Bullen. She had always hated the man and her dislike was patent now in that quick, penetrating glance.

'I do not rely on anyone's evidence unless it is substantiated,' Bill said. 'You see, I know *why* you came here that evening.'

'*No!*' The quick negative seemed to be wrung from her.

'I'm sorry to have to distress you, Miss Jax, but you came here for the one purpose of trying to obtain a certain photograph . . . '

'All right — I did then, but it was *my* property. *Mine*, I tell you, and I didn't get it, anyway. Mrs Letts would not even open the door to me.'

'Do you remember what time you came that evening?'

'I . . . I don't know. About half past six, I suppose.'

Abruptly Bill turned to Mr Bullen. 'Is

that the time *you* saw Miss Jax arrive at
The Elms? he asked.

'I told you before — it was about five
and twenty to seven. I went there myself
about twenty past six. Saw *her* go in just
after . . . when I'd been back over
home . . . '

Bill turned again to Gwenda. 'When
you said Mrs Letts would not open the
door to you, do you mean you could not
get any answer to your knock?'

'No, she had a chain on the door. She
opened it wide enough to speak to me.
But she said she was busy and had no
time for visitors.'

'Mrs Letts was obviously a cautious
woman.' Bill Rice stroked his eyebrow
with his forefinger for several seconds.
Gwenda said into the silence, 'I told her
what I wanted — but she wouldn't let me
in.'

Bill did not appear to hear her. He was
looking at Tiny Bullen. He said quietly,
'There was one person Mrs Letts would
allow into her home without any query
— one person who had been here many
times. I put it to you that you came here,

259

not *before* Miss Jax but *afterwards*.'

Tiny did not speak. He was watching Bill as though mesmerized.

'The woman who had worked for you was leaving . . . '

'She is still with me,' Mr Bullen put in then.

'Oh, I know — but you had to raise her wages considerably in order to keep her,' Bill stated, and suddenly Tiny's eyes were full of venom.

'You low-down, snooping bastard!' he ejaculated, but Bill kept on, 'The day that Mrs Letts died your woman had given in her notice because she said you did not pay her enough. You thought that *now* you had to make the widow over the road see sense. *She* could come and look after you, leaving her daughter and the lodger to fend for themselves. I suggest *that* part of what you told me was true. You *did* talk to her about the casserole. You put out every persuasion you could think of to make Mrs Letts agree to marry you very quickly, and move into your home before anyone knew anything about it. In fact, you were so sure that you would get your way that you had bought a special licence . . . '

'No!' It was Madeline who gave the low incredulous exclamation. Tiny glanced at her and in the same moment put a hand up to his moustache in that nervous gesture which was almost part of himself. He looked as though between his half-open lips there was a word — a very nasty word which he wanted to spit in Bill's direction. But my friend forestalled him. He said, 'You couldn't really believe that, when it came to the point, any woman like Mrs Letts would turn you down flat. But she did. She told you to take yourself off — be about your business and leave her alone — for good and all.'

I saw the tip of Bullen's tongue run along between his lips but he did not speak.

Bill went on, 'You were mad — crazily mad in that moment, even though normally you are a gentle person. The stick was on the table. You picked it up . . . '

'No!' Again it was Madeline who spoke

into the hush as Bill paused, but the next moment he was asking, 'Do you deny this, Mr Bullen?'

Still the man did not reply and Bill added, 'Your fingerprints were on the weapon which murdered Mrs Letts . . . '

This was something which Bill had not told *me*. He was going on relentlessly, '*You* knew there was a key on the ledge inside the front door. You knew it was easy enough to slip along the passage and outside, locking the door behind you.'

'It isn't true,' Tiny burst out. 'You are making this all up — reconstructing the crime — but you can't *prove* anything . . . '

'We have proved your fingerprints on the stick *and* another thing — that door key was found right in the middle of your holly arch. You thought no one would ever find it there. 'You wouldn't think anybody would muck about with prickly holly' — *you* said that to Dr. Jax.'

'In *my* arch . . . Then it was . . . the police . . . That day I went to them, but they never told me it was *their* men had ruined my lovely holly. They did it while I was out of the way . . . '

'Yes — and you suspected they had found the key, didn't you? You thought it would appear less suspicious if you went along and reported it. Perhaps you even felt it would be easier to *grasp* the nettle, thinking that, when you got to the station, they would tell you they had found the key . . . '

'No, no! It's not that way at all,' Tiny interrupted. 'I *didn't* know anything about that key — nor did I kill Mrs Letts either. Oh yes, I was mad with her. I did touch that stick — I remember doing it — but I never intended to hit her — I would never have harmed a hair of her head. I just caught hold of that stick as it lay on the table — for support, almost.'

He gripped both hands together. 'Now laugh, all you younger folk. Someone retired — someone as old as I am being in love! Funny, you think — but it's true. I loved Emma Letts — it wasn't any different from when I was in my teens. I couldn't sleep for thinking about her. I never wanted to go far from my window in case I'd miss getting a glimpse of her.

And she would have had me. That night I was sure of it. She *wanted* to get away from this bungalow but she *dared* not. I don't know *why* but she was afraid of something or someone . . . '

'That's enough, Mr Bullen. I have a great more to say and our time is precious.'

I had known Bill a long time but, until recently, never in his official capacity. He seemed suddenly to have changed from a cheery friend into a harsh, insensitive stranger.

He was talking to John Harvey now. '*You*,' he said, 'are Mrs Letts' stepson.'

I saw Madeline turn quickly to look at Harvey. She was obviously taken aback by the statement but she said nothing. Harvey asked in a harsh voice, 'How did you find that out?'

'Quite easily. Old Mr Underhill lived next door to your father and Mrs Letts when they first came to Mewsdale — and then they had a boy with them, but only for a week or two. Your stepmother said the child was a son of her sister who was emigrating. It was not difficult to check up records and discover the truth.'

'Your father married again after your own mother died — and the new Mrs Letts was jealous of you. And soon you hated her. She had you sent to a home — even registered you under a different name because she wanted you to have no claim on your father. You never forgave her — always it rankled at the back of your mind.'

Bill paused, waiting perhaps for Harvey to deny those dogmatic statements. But the other man remained silent, his hands thrust deep into his pockets.

At last Bill went on, 'Some time ago you returned to this town, walked along this road — and in at the gate of a house on the opposite side from this. It was the house where you knew your father had once lived. You knocked at the door. You had steeled yourself to face the woman you hated — but it was a young woman who answered you. When you asked how long she had lived there she told you quite a while. Then you enquired about the folk before her, and she said they had gone to Leeds.'

'And I went there,' Harvey said in a low tone.

'It never occured to you that a house might have a whole succession of tenants,' Bill remarked, 'and I can only imagine you could not bring yourself to mention Mrs Letts by name — or you would have been told that she lived only just across the road. It must have come as a great surprise to you when you realized that is just what had happened.' Again Bill paused, but Harvey said nothing, and the relentless voice began again.

'Then you met Ralph Tennant and, by a strange coincidence, he had rooms in your stepmother's home. You saw her and knew she had recognized you from your likeness to your father. You left here on that fatal evening — but you came back to get your revenge . . . '

Harvey had remained leaning back in his chair all the time Bill was talking. Now suddenly he sat forward. 'It's true she was my stepmother,' he admitted, 'and that all my life I have hated her. But I didn't kill her. I told you the truth. Madeline dropped me at the station and I caught the . . . train to London.'

'Do you still insist, Miss Letts, that Mr Harvey is not telling the truth?' Bill looked now at Madeline, who unfolded her arms and gripped the side of the settee with one hand. 'Of course I insist,' she said.

'And suppose I have evidence to prove he is *not* lying? That, in fact, you *did* drop him at the railway station . . . '

'I don't care how much evidence you've got. I drove Ralph to Tonsford that evening. The lecture began at seven thirty sharp. You can check with the twenty people in the class that we were both there.

'We have already done that, Miss Letts, and so the alibi for you and Mr Tennant is corroborated very apparently.'

I saw Madeline relax, watched her hand loosen its grip on the settee, and again I felt angry with Bill for his treatment of her. Then she glanced at Harvey and I was sure it was triumph I saw in her eyes. Almost I could read her thought — So *I* am safe — but you are not . . .

No, he had a motive, and what could

be more cruel than hate? He was still lying, too, about having gone on that train. I looked across at him, still sitting up alertly in his chair. But the expression on his dark closed face told me nothing. 'One of you murdered her . . . ' And Harvey was the man who thought killing could confer a favour on the victim — the excitement of seeing what lay beyond death . . .

Bill was speaking now to Mrs Hodgson, but she refused to look at him, appeared not to hear his questions. After several minutes he gave up trying and turned his attention to Nurse Mackail.

I could sympathise with Mrs Hodgson almost as much as I did with Madeline for, after all, the whole affair was nothing to do with her. She had not known Mrs Letts and had certainly been nowhere in the vicinity of Mewsdale when the murder took place.

Once more Bill's voice cut across the silence of the room. 'Nurse Mackail, *why* did you move the body? What were you trying to hide?'

'Nothing,' she insisted but without

looking at her interrogator.

'I will tell you something. Instead of hiding anything you revealed a vital clue — something which in your hurry you did not notice. Under Mrs Letts' body was a photograph — the very one which Miss Jax had, on the previous evening, tried to obtain.'

I heard Gwenda gasp, saw her fingers loosen on the gloves so that they dropped to the floor. I leaned over and picked them up, touching her hand as I gave them back to her. She gave me a quick grateful smile but it was a smile which did not reach her eyes.

There was a stifled sob and I realized that the nurse was crying. Madeline, Gwenda, Tiny Bullen — all of them had kept their feelings under control, but Nurse Mackail had given way beneath the detective's questioning. He was saying, 'I will tell you what happened on the night of the murder, Nurse. You were attending Mr Underhill across the road and as you came out after your visit you saw the light switched off in this bungalow. You know all the medical evidence revealing the approximate time of Mrs Letts' death. You know who the murderer is.'

Gwenda leaned suddenly against me and I slipped my arm across her shoulders. Madeline tensed in her chair, folding her arms again and gripping her forearms tightly. Mr Bullen ground his heel into the carpet, and Mrs Hodgson remained quite motionless in her chair.

Bill reached for a chair and sat down. 'I am going to tell you a story,' he said. 'It is about two people and it took place some time ago in a huge building a long way from this bungalow.'

15

No one stirred, no one spoke as Bill added slowly, 'We shall call these two X and Y for the moment. One of them might be a woman . . . '

That last sentence caused a ripple of movement in the room. Tennant glanced round at Madeline but she was huddled in her corner of the settee, eyes closed, her breathing deep. Almost she might be asleep.

Harvey's gaze lifted to dart across the room at Gwenda, and I knew she was conscious of those dark, unfriendly eyes. She gripped my hand tightly.

Tiny Bullen looked up — first at Nurse Mackail and then at Mrs Hodgson. It might have been that he needed to feel the assurance of the chair arms under his hands. At any rate, instead of tugging at his moustache, he thrust out his lower lip with a sudden sucking noise which seemed very loud in the silent room.

Nurse Mackail was still crying silently, unaware of who might be surveying her. Mrs Hodgson could have been made of stone — so quiet and immobile she sat on her chair.

I am sure Bill was aware of the reactions of each of us before he went on, 'Now, one evening X had an appointment and kept it. There was no reason why he should not, for he had made the arrangement himself. But things did not work out the way he expected, and he left a dead body behind him.

'X was evil but, up to that date, his crimes had never included murder. Fortunately for him, during the whole of that interview, he wore gloves so there were no fingerprints of his anywhere in the room. No one knew he was in any way connected with the person he had killed — or that he had previously made an appointment with him. So if he could manage to get out of the building where he had committed the brutal act, he would be safe.

'Unluckily for him — or rather luckily as it transpired later, there was someone else in the place other than himself. He had almost reached the outer doors of the building — only a few more moments and he would be free . . .

'He was crossing a wide foyer with doors on both sides of it. Suddenly one of them opened and someone — Y, came out. X and Y were both surprised to see one another, for each believed himself to be the only person in the building. Or should we say X thought he was the only one *alive* — for he had the guilty knowledge that, in a room two flights of stairs up, there was a dead body.'

Then Bill Rice hesitated, waiting perhaps for some reaction from the people in the room. But no one moved. Again, in the sudden, uncanny silence I was conscious of the ticking of that ornate clock on the mantelpiece before Bill's voice once more took up the tale.

'Imagine it — a murderer faced by another person who would now know he had been in the building — who would be able to describe him. Then, suddenly, he knew that Y was a heaven-sent opportunity — though 'heaven-sent' does not seem quite the right expression. Y was wearing overalls and it was quite apparent that he worked in the place, but it was very large, and so the chance was very great that he would not know everyone else who worked there. X, putting this sudden idea to the test, said, 'I have just come from the Managing Director's office. He wanted to see me this evening about the latest import order. I have just remembered — I've left my brief case in his room. I wonder if you would mind fetching it for me? We didn't agree on several points and I don't want to see him again till he has simmered down a bit.'

'The only truth in that speech was that X and the managing director — who was the murdered person — had not agreed about several things. But of course Y did not know that. He took it for granted that the smartly-dressed X was one of the firm's directors.

'Without any hesitation Y went to fetch the brief case. When he reached the managing director's office he knocked and, receiving no reply, knocked louder. Eventually he turned the handle and went in. Apparently no one was there nor, from his position in the doorway, could he see any brief case. He walked across to the huge desk, moved a chair to see if the brief case had fallen beneath it and then went to the other side of the desk. He stopped suddenly. He grasped the desk edge to steady himself. He seemed to be, all at once, in the middle of a horrific nightmare.

'There at his feet lay the Managing Director — face downwards on the thick carpet. His head had been cruelly bashed in, and the implement which had caused the injuries lay beyond him — a heavy glass ash tray set in a thick metal surround.

'Y stood there for perhaps a couple of seconds then, possibly thinking he might be able to do something, he bent down and tugged the body over on its back. He knew, as he looked at the white set face that the other man was beyond help. Murder — brutal, cruel murder had been done.'

I found myself glancing at Nurse Mackail. *She* had found the body of Mrs

Letts and moved it — putting it face upwards on the bed. Was there some connection between her action and that of the person Bill had just told about?

But if there was she gave no sign. She had stopped crying and now sat silently in her chair, her handkerchief held against her eyes. I brought my attention back from the nurse to Gwenda, as I felt her hand creep into mine. I realized that Bill's story was affecting her deeply — yet what could it have to do with Gwenda?

I did not even know if what he was telling was the truth or just some hypothetical case. Worried about my sister, wondering if I could make some excuse to get her away from the room, it was almost a relief to hear Bill's voice again.

He went on, 'Suddenly Y realized his predicament. And, like many others before him, he panicked. He went out of the director's office and down two flights of stairs at about a tenth of the speed he had gone up them. X was no longer in the foyer, but he had not really expected to find him. Y fetched his coat, put it on, switched off the lights and left the building. As he went down the outside steps another member of the staff who knew him quite well saw him and greeted him, remarking on the fact that it was unusual for Y to be working so late.

'Y scarcely replied to him, but shrugged his collar up round his face and hurried away. When he arrived home he panicked even more. He found that some of the murdered man's blood was on his shirt sleeve and carefully washed it out.

'He realized that to run away would make him look guilty, so he went to work as usual next morning. He was not surprised to find the place swarming with police and detectives. The fingerprints of everyone on the staff were taken and, later that day, Y was arrested and charged with murder. You see, it was so obvious he had done it. His fingerprints were on the desk and chair in the Managing Director's office where he had no right at all to be. He was only a maintenance man and had been there that evening to see about a fault in the central heating system.

'Then there was the testimony of a

work-mate who had seen him leave the building just after the time medical evidence assessed as that of the murdered man's death. And, although he had washed his shirt, the forensic laboratory found traces of blood of the same group as the director's on his overalls.

'Y's defence was the truth — that the man who was the murderer had been leaving the building just as Y had been coming through the foyer and had asked him to go and fetch a mythical brief case. But, against all the damning evidence there was only Y's word.

'Of course he described the man he had seen, yet all he could really tell was that he was taller than himself and smartly dressed.

'Y was convicted of murder.'

I felt Gwenda's hand tremble in mine but, other than that, she did not move. I glanced again at the other occupants of the room.

Tennant had put the antelope head down on the settee between himself and Madeline, and was sitting forward, hands clasped above his knees. John Harvey had one hand in his mouth and was biting his nails with a vicious concentration which sent shivers down my spine. I guessed Madeline shared my distaste for she was watching him angrily as though she would like to tell him to stop.

Tiny Bullen opened his mouth and closed it again. It must be agony for *him* to sit there all this time not saying anything, I thought.

'Meanwhile,' Bill continued, 'X was delighted. His quickly thought-out plan had been successful. He was completely free and someone else would pay the penalty for his crime. But X was a man of many parts. Not only had he escaped from the consequences of his crime but he planned to make money from it — and fate was kind to him. He was passing a photographer's window just a day or two after his crime when he noticed a picture. His quick brain was instantly alert. He stepped into the shop and asked if he could buy the print. The man who ran the photographic studio was a person of more principle than X. He knew that one of the people in that photograph had been charged with murder, and not wishing to make money out of someone else's misfortune, had fully intended to remove the likeness from the window. Perhaps quite naturally he suspected that X might be a reporter.

'But X was very charming, with a persuasive way of talking. He explained that he was a relative of one of the folk in the print and eventually the photographer sold it to him.'

Bill stopped. Suddenly. And looked at Gwenda.

'Perhaps,' he said, 'you would like to go on from there, Miss Jax.'

I held my arm closer round Gwenda's shoulder. I was even more angry with Bill — and determined to tell him just what I thought of him. But I had only got as far as the first angry syllable when I felt my sister's other hand close over mine.

'It's all right, Ian,' she said quietly. 'I have tried to keep this from you, but I know now how wrong I have been.' Then in a slightly louder tone she said, looking at Bill, 'My husband's name is James Royce.'

There was a quick gasp from several people in the room. Obviously the name meant more to them than it did to me. Again I seemed to hear the windscreen wiper as I drove home several days ago. The way its rhythm repeated to me, 'James . . . Royce . . .'

Gwenda's tone was now agitated but clear. 'My husband was convicted of murder. But he is innocent. *I* always knew he was. But no one else believed him. *No one*. I had to keep it from my family — from you, Ian. I couldn't let you know that your brother-in-law was a convicted murderer . . .'

Poor unhappy Gwenda. All these months she had lived with her secret. If only she had shared it with me — how much unhappiness and worry we might both have been saved.

Bill got up from his chair and walked across to stand near her. 'Please believe me, I have not wanted to distress you like this, but would you tell us what happened when *you* went to that photographer's?'

I realized that from his new position

Bill could watch everyone in the room more easily and also that he was standing between all of us and the door.

I wanted to tell Gwenda that she need not reply, that we would go home straightaway. I regretted that I had allowed her to come.

But she seemed to have forgotten me. For the first time she looked round at the other people, at Madeline and Ralph Tennant, Nurse Mackail and John Harvey, at Tiny Bullen and Mrs Hodgson. Finally her glance came back to Bill Rice himself.

'I don't care if they do know now,' she said. 'James — my husband could never have done such a terrible thing.'

'I think we may be able to prove his innocence now,' Bill said, 'but first I want you to tell us what happened at the photographer's when you visited the studio several days after your husband had been charged with murder.'

'I . . . I . . . did not want my folk to know. My parents were against James right from the start. He was a manual worker, and they thought that, as a doctor's daughter with a college education behind me, I should marry further up the social scale. So we married secretly and then . . . then . . . '

Bill waited for a few seconds. 'Then, when he was charged with murder, you felt you could not possibly reveal that you had married him . . . '

Gwenda nodded. 'We had been married only a fortnight when the dreadful thing happened. Of course I went to the court — but the newspaper men never realized who I was and so I didn't have their cameras trained on me, and during the trial I was not mentioned. James, determined that I should not be brought into it, kept our secret. And then I remembered our wedding photos. I had got a man in a little shop in Cleand to take one because, although I was married secretly, I wanted a record of that, for me, happy day. I was determined that when James had made a position for himself I would show that picture to my parents.'

Her voice faltered. 'You remembered the photo,' Bill prompted.

'Yes, I went to the studio and asked the

man if I could buy the proofs and negative. I could not risk a newspaper getting hold of them. Well, he let me have them — but he told me that someone he had thought at first to be a reporter had bought a print from him the previous day, saying he was a relative of mine.'

Again her voice faltered before she added, 'I knew of course that it could not have been a relation and the photographer's description conveyed nothing to me. For days afterwards I was worried. I pored through all the newspapers dreading to see the photograph that would let my parents know I had married James.'

'But the picture was never published?' Bill said.

'No.'

'And it did not occur to you to link the person who had bought your photograph with the description which your huband had given of the man he had seen on the night of the murder?'

'Why should I connect the two? James' description was very vague — the photographer's quite detailed because he had talked to the man and been only a counter's width away from him.'

Bill was silent for a few moments before he said, 'In fact the two descriptions belong to one and the same person. And, because of the unusual circumstances, the photographer in Cleand can still remember accurately and in great detail everything about the person who bought that photograph. His description fits someone in this room today . . . someone who used that photograph for the despicable crime of blackmail . . . someone who, because he had got away with one murder, thought it would be possible to escape the consequences of a second one, even perhaps a third . . . '

Bill's voice was clear and firm. 'We know now that the person who murdered the Managing Director of the Greet Electra Company also murdered Mrs Letts. In both cases the crimes were committed in exactly the same way. In both cases the murderer had been blackmailing the victim. In both cases he lost his temper, strode in anger across the room and back again. Both times he picked up the nearest heavy instrument and bashed his victim's head in, an ash tray in the case of the Director, a heavily carved stick in the other. Mrs Letts looked after Mr Tennant's rooms and, unfortunately for her that evening, she intended to polish up his collection of sticks.

'She came into this room to fetch them soon after all the visitors had gone and it was then that she saw this photograph, remembering that Miss Jax had come to the door only minutes earlier to say she wanted to fetch a photo from Mr Tennant's room . . . '

Bill suddenly held up the photograph I had given him and which I knew now was of Gwenda and James Royce. He said, 'It had obviously been left behind by one of the people who were in this room during the afternoon. Mrs Letts recognized both the people in the print and carried it back with her to the kitchen — possibly to look at it more closely. She put one of the sticks ready for polishing on the table and the rest on the floor. She was bending to look at the photograph when there was a movement behind her . . . '

Bill's glance went to Tiny Bullen. He said, 'Mr Bullen *had* called but had not been encouraged to stay. There was quite a lot of work to be done after Mr Tennant's entertaining. Miss Jax came to the door and *she* was not admitted. As far as Mrs Letts knew Mr Tennant, Mr Harvey, Dr Jax and Madeline had all left the bungalow quite a while earlier. So when she heard a movement behind her she was startled.'

When Bill paused I thought he was waiting for someone to make a movement — to try to escape perhaps. But no one moved. Bodies were rigid, expressions strained. Even Tiny Bullen had stopped grinding the heel of his shoe in the carpet. It was as if we were all petrified and only Bill could release us from the spell. He went on, 'Mrs Letts knew the figure which stood in the doorway. She was astonished — yet perhaps not too surprised for she had seen this person many times and hated him as only a blackmailer *can* be hated. She saw the glance sent at the photograph in her hand — saw the expression on his face and knew at once that it was property she was not supposed to see, and that it had been used for the very same reason as a secret of her own had been used — for blackmail. That night more money was to be demanded from her.

'Mrs Letts possibly said, 'You mean skunk — you coward — battening on defenceless women. Well, you've had all I possess. I've nothing else to give you.'

'The murderer's temper was roused. He strode across the room and back — as he always did when he was angry. He saw the stick on the table. He picked it up, raised it, and as it was brought down Mrs Letts turned her head and received a glancing blow on her temple. She turned away, but pitilessly the stick descended again — on the back of her head now. Perhaps only *then* the monster realized what he had done.

'Flight was necessary — and as quickly as possible, but first there was some clearing up to be achieved. Perhaps it *might* look like an accident . . .

'In his haste he completely forgot the photograph which had fluttered to the ground beneath his victim. It was still there the next day and Dr Jax found it.

'The murderer switched off the light before he went out through the front door, as James Royce had done from a different building many months ago. And, as James Royce happened to be seen by someone who knew him so X, who had commited this second murder, was seen by someone who knew *him*.'

He paused, turning slightly away from us all as he did so. 'It's very much like that picture,' he said, 'the tiger killing the antelope and the man killing the tiger — a somehow inevitable sequence . . .'

He shrugged and turned back to us. 'As I was saying, our murderer reached the gateway of this bungalow just as someone was leaving the house opposite. That someone was Nurse Mackail.'

Bill looked across at her. 'Why did you try to shield this person who committed this terrible crime? Why did you move the body, perhaps destroying vital clues in doing so? Why did you insist it was an accident when it was so patently murder? *Who* are you shielding, Nurse? Was it a man or a woman who left the bungalow that night? Who was it, Nurse Mackail — *who?*'

She spoke in a smothered voice. 'The one I saw . . . Next morning I remembered I'd seen him but I was sure he could not have done the awful thing. I was afraid, though, that he would be blamed — if I said anything . . . '

'But who was it?' Bill insisted.

She took the handkerchief from her eyes then, looked up, across the room . . .

And then it happened. Bill must surely have been expecting it, yet even he was not prepared for so quick a movement. The man was across the room in three swift bounds, pushing Bill aside and forcing himself through the doorway.

'It's no good.' Bill shouted the warning. 'This place is surrounded. Police are all round the bungalow.'

I was conscious of Gwenda, her resistance broken at last, sobbing against me. In a blurred sort of way I saw the others rush past me into the hall. Only Mrs Hodgson remained sullen and unspeaking on her chair.

Gwenda looked up at me. 'I wish I had told you, Ian. You see, he was blackmailing me, too. But for Dad's sake — for yours since you came home — how could I let anyone know I was married to someone convicted of murder?'

'It doesn't matter now, Gwenda,' I told her. 'We will talk about it when we get home.' I pulled her to her feet, anxious to get her away from this room and its horrible, leering contents. But as I did so there was the sound of a shot, followed by a scream.

16

My sister had suffered enough during the past months. I did not want her to be distressed any more, but I was a doctor. If anyone was hurt I must go to them. 'Stay here,' I said, 'I will be back as soon as possible.'

I went quickly into the hall. I heard voices in the kitchen, a babble of excited and terrified voices and, above them, Bill's.

I pushed into the room — the small shabby room which had witnessed now a second violent death. For he was quite dead. After all, shooting had been part of his livelihood. And the last shot — the one he had fired into his own brain when he knew he was trapped — was perhaps the most accurate shot of all. Ralph Tennant — hunter, blackmailer, murderer. And yet people had been captivated by him. Madeline and Nurse Mackail knelt by his side sobbing . . .

Bill was ordering everyone out of the room, opening the outer door to admit two burly policemen. I heard Nurse Mackail say to Madeline, 'Come along to my home.' I watched them go arm-in-arm along the hall and out of the front door.

Just inside the hall I stood with Bill as I said, 'Whoever shot him that day was another of his blackmail victims, I suppose — someone who hated him.'

'No,' Bill replied. 'It was the picture which solved that for me.'

'The picture?' I repeated, thinking at once of Gwenda's wedding photo. Fear gripped my heart again. Had Gwenda . . . ? But his next words dissolved my fear.

'The picture on Tennant's wall,' he explained. 'You see, when he came in and found me looking at it that day he told me the man had shot the tiger.'

'Well, what about it? The man was holding a rifle and the animal was quite obviously dead.' I glanced up and saw that he was smiling — that enigmatical smile of his.

'Come and take another look at it,' he said. 'I have to go and ring up for the ambulance, anyway.'

We left the two policemen in charge of the body. When we got to the sitting room Gwenda was no longer there and, glancing out of the window, I saw she was in the back seat of the car. To my surprise, Mrs Hodgson was beside her. There was no one else there — even Harvey had not returned to complete his task — both he and Tiny Bullen had disappeared.

I followed Bill across the carpet and stood looking up at the painting. I must admit I had not really examined it before. 'You see,' Bill said. 'The tiger was not shot.'

'There appears to be some sort of spear arrangement protruding from its back,' I replied, 'but I still don't understand.'

'Anyone who had not taken an interest in hunting would probably not realise the significance of that spear,' he told me. 'It's a very cruel way some of the African natives have of killing animals. It is a spear fixed to a heavy log. There is a trip cord attached to it and then it's edged into the branches of a tree. Some poor unsuspecting animal comes along, touches the cord and, hey presto, the spear comes crashing down into its back.'

'Whatever has that got to do with anyone shooting Tennant?' I asked.

'Everything,' Bill replied. 'I knew *he* must realize how the animal in that picture had died and I wondered why he should say it was shot — why not just say it was killed? Then, when I asked you about the time of the shooting that afternoon, you obviously thought Tennant had phoned Gore about twenty past five — while you were attending to Madeline. In fact, the call was entered as having been received at the station at five-forty-five.'

I turned away from the cruel picture. I still couldn't follow what he was trying to tell me.

'Tennant wanted those minutes,' he was saying. 'It was important he should have some time after you left and before the police arrived. He had fixed a gun in the tree that afternoon before you reached here.'

'And was just returning from the

garden when I arrived a quarter of an hour early . . . Are you telling me that he rigged up that gun on the same principle as those trap spears just to kill himself — with me as a witness?'

'Not to *kill* himself — merely to make it appear as though someone was trying to do so. He was a very clever man, Ian. When you heard what you thought might be someone among the trees, it was him touching the trip cord. Actually he did not intend to get hurt at all. He thought just the fact of someone shooting *at* him would throw the police off the scent — and make them look elsewhere for the murderer. *I* had been here to question him and Madeline — he thought I was getting far too nosey, so he staged his own 'murder' attempt.'

'It completely took me in,' I admitted, 'especially when we saw Tiny Bullen. Then it *was* his dog we heard go into the water?'

'Yes, that was quite a bit of luck for Tennant. His ruse worked very well. He only had to go back down the garden path after you had gone, remove the gun and toss it into the pond, destroy the trip cord — and then come back to ring up Gore. He had sustained an injury but that was likely to put the police even more off the trail, and he probably thought it well worthwhile.'

I saw him glance through the window at Gwenda sitting patiently in the car. 'I'm sorry I had to distress her, Ian,' he said, 'but today is *really* a happy one for her. I can supply plenty of evidence to prove her husband innocent.'

I knew he was right. In time we should all forget these terrible weeks.

Bill was saying, '*If* Tennant thought the police did not investigate the back way out after Mrs Letts' death, he must have thought them a very inefficient lot! *That* morning the grass in the garden was completely undisturbed and there was no scrap of tweed on the wire.'

I began to walk away and Bill picked up the handset of the telephone. In the doorway I paused, waiting for him to finish. Then I said, 'There are still two points that you have not cleared up for me. Tennant *was* at Tonsford that night.'

'Yes, but Madeline did not drive him. Have you forgotten there is an airport handy? You complain enough about interference from the planes.'

'And she was prepared to swear blind that she drove him up.'

'Even invented about asking him whether he had switched off the light so as to make it sound more convincing,' Bill said. '*She* knew Tennant did not get all his money on the level and imagined he did some sort of a fiddle with the customs.'

'And Nurse Mackail,' I asked, 'why did you say there could be another murder when I told you about seeing her with Tennant near the river?'

'Because I could guess what she was telling him — that she had seen him on the night of the murder — and she was probably pleading with him to reassure her he had not done the dreadful deed . . . ' Bill paused.

'Tennant was a very charming man to women — when he chose to be. Both the nurse and Madeline Letts were infatuated with him. Insidiously *he* had planted the idea in Madeline's mind that it was necessary for her to raise a mortage on the bungalow — she was beginning to arrange it . . . '

* * *

When I reached the car Gwenda was alone. She said, 'Tiny Bullen realized Mrs Hodgson was in the car with me just now. He came over and invited her to have a cup of tea with him. It might be a good thing if those two made a match of it — Tiny being so garrulous and Mrs H. so silent they should make a very good pair!' I saw the laughter in her eyes again — this was more like the sister I used to know. I put my hand over hers. 'I'm so glad everything is going to be all right,' I said.

'Yes, everything's going to be all right,' Gwenda repeated slowly, 'not only for myself and you — and Dad, but for many other people. It is terrible to think how many lives a really wicked person can ruin. I suppose nearly everyone has a secret in their past . . . Tennant made it his business to search out the skeletons from the cupboards and, if his victims had no money, he used his knowledge to force them into unwilling service for him. That's the explanation for Mrs Letts having her bungalow smartened up for him and afterwards waiting on him. I guess she hated Madeline for taking him there.'

I slipped the car into gear and drew away from the pavement. 'And Mrs Hodgson,' Gwenda went on. 'He forced *her* to come and look after Madeline as well as himself.'

'You mean he blackmailed her into it?'

'That's right. She has just told me so. She didn't give me any details — just said in that reedy voice of hers that she was glad Tennant was dead — that now the past would never be able to hurt her again.'

We were both silent, perhaps both of us thinking that we, too, were glad that such an influence had been removed from our lives.

Dad was standing just inside the gate when we arrived home. I wondered if he had been watching for us. 'You have been gone a long time,' he said.

I think he knew we had a great deal to tell him, and I did not know where to start. 'Come on into the sitting room,' I said.

Within a short time all three of us were sitting in chairs round the fireside and there we pieced together the whole story of the past distressing months. Ralph Tennant had first blackmailed my mother with the threat that he would reveal Gwenda's marriage. Mum, afraid of the scandal that she thought would ruin Dad's practice, paid him again and again. When the worry of it had eventually driven her to take her own life the man had turned to Dad — threatening to have the photograph published in the news-papers, together with the story of Gwenda's 'romance with a murderer'.

Swift bitterness swept over me. I had been *friendly* with the monster who had virtually killed my mother and impover-ished my father . . .

Then, not content with that, on the day when Dad and I returned to find him leaving the house, he had begun to blackmail Gwenda herself — and she had paid him several amounts. When Bill and I watched her go to that car — it *was* Tennant's and she had just come from the bank. He had threatened to reveal her secret to Dad . . .

I saw them look at one another — if only they had confided in each other — and in me. If only Gwenda had told me the truth on the morning when I came on her reading that letter. She confessed now it had been from her husband. He wrote regularly and she knew just when to expect his letters — and always, till the morning when I decided to get up early, she had been downstairs first.

★　★　★

It has helped to write this story, to share it with others. Now, a year later, it all seems like some violent nightmare.

Gwenda no longer lives at Roseville, as she has her own home a short distance away. Her husband was released and he is all I could wish for in a brother-in-law.

He has taken on a business which he is building into a thriving concern — carrying out maintenance jobs of every description. *He* has installed central heating and an efficient hot water system in our house and surgery.

Dad, once more his old cheerful self, is the more active half of the partnership now. I suppose I could go back to my hospital life, but somehow I don't think I will . . .

THE END

We do hope that you have enjoyed reading this large print book.

Did you know that all of our titles are available for purchase?

We publish a wide range of high quality large print books including:
Romances, Mysteries, Classics
General Fiction
Non Fiction and Westerns

Special interest titles available in large print are:
The Little Oxford Dictionary
Music Book, Song Book
Hymn Book, Service Book

Also available from us courtesy of Oxford University Press:
Young Readers' Dictionary
(large print edition)
Young Readers' Thesaurus
(large print edition)

For further information or a free brochure, please contact us at:
Ulverscroft Large Print Books Ltd.,
The Green, Bradgate Road, Anstey,
Leicester, LE7 7FU, England.
Tel: (00 44) **0116 236 4325**
Fax: (00 44) **0116 234 0205**